ORIGINAL FINISH

BOOKS BY JACK GUNTER

Wally Winchester Adventures:
   Original Finish
   The Egg Rocker
   Mother of God

*A Pictorial History of the Pacific Northwest
Including the Future*

The Gunter Papers

ORIGINAL FINISH

JACK GUNTER

A WALLY WINCHESTER ADVENTURE

Flying Pig Publications
Camano Island, Washington
flyngpig@camano.net

This novel is a work of fiction. Names, characters, places, and incidents either are products of the author's imagination or are products of historical record or geographic descriptions used fictitiously. Any resemblance to actual persons, living or dead, is pure coincidence.

Copyright © 2010 by Jack Gunter

ISBN 13: 978-0-9841841-0-1
ISBN 10: 0-9841841-0-4

Printed in the United States of America by Ingram Books

Prelude

The angry crowd was getting louder, closer. Elizabeth Moffatt saw the flickering lanterns careening toward the ship from beyond the docks and merchant storerooms at Newport Harbor. Dull red incandescence glowed from the direction of their home. Foul-scented deck hands grunted and pulled on the lines as they raised the last piece of furniture to the slightly rolling deck's level. "Thomas, they're coming. We must leave now."

"I'm not leaving this dock, Elizabeth, without that desk," her husband said. He seemed unconcerned about the commotion about to erupt at the end of the pier. "Careful, you louts! You'll bugger the finish!"

The cargo net swung wildly as the last of the household mahogany was hoisted over the side toward the open cargo hold. The sailors were also anxious to cast off the lines and get safely underway.

"Damn you and your furniture, Thomas Moffatt," she said. "Our family is in danger. Your practice is in ruins. Our neighbors hate us. They want to HANG you. And all you can think about is your precious Chippendale!"

Elizabeth was taken aback by her own insolence, but she was well past caring about propriety. After Thomas had spoken in favor of the British, the preceding months had been miserable. None of her friends had spoken to her since Thomas publicly stated his views. The children had been harassed by other children. Once, young Tom had come home covered with bruises, his clothes torn. If they escaped the angry citizens approaching the dock, they would be heading into the frightening Atlantic Ocean toward an uncertain future in a cold, remote Canadian village in Nova Scotia. No, I had every right, even as a wife, she thought, to exhibit my disapproval. Thomas Moffatt's bold tongue had ruined a perfect life in Newport, Rhode Island, and his obsession with three pieces of furniture was about to get them killed.

The three-masted frigate floated free as the lines were pulled away from the dock, and angry shouts crossed the widening gap of darkness.

"Go home, you Tory bastards!"

"England deserves you, traitors!"

Moffatt didn't hear his neighbors' catcalls. He was in the hold, ministering to the safety of his desk.

It will be a cold day in Halifax before I grace your bed again, Thomas Moffatt, Elizabeth thought, listening to his endless fussing from below decks.

Her eyes wet with tears, she looked back at the starlit, receding New England shoreline. A freshening breeze caught the mainsail and pushed the little ship into the dubious safety of the dark sea beyond.

Elizabeth Moffatt turned away from America as the conflagration leapt into the sky, destroying her home on the shore.

Customs Inspection, International Ferry Dock, Port Angeles, Washington, 230 Years Later

The customs agent saw the elderly traveler's eyes wander. He looked nervous. Unfocused. His hand twitched as he handed a Canadian passport over.

"Anything to declare, Mr. Smith?" The traveler was just one in the long line of vehicles exiting the ferry from Victoria, BC. A bright sodium arc in the halide lights on the ceiling bathed the red van in a green-yellow glow.

"Just some junk from a yard sale," the driver mumbled. Head bowed, he glanced furtively intot the outside mirror at the line behind him. He extracted a folded document from a worn-out wallet and handed it out the half-open window.

The inspector penned a note on the document and passed it back. "Pull over to the first bay to the right and bring this form inside," Agent Thomas said.

"Sir, I'm in a hurry. I have to get to Tacoma by five. Can you just take a look inside and pass me through?"

"Drive to bay number one, please." Thomas pressed a red button on his console.

"Get back in there, Cujo," the dog handler said. The black-and-white terrier bounded into the van through the open back doors and clambered over the pile inside, then jumped down calmly and walked to his handler's side, tail wagging.

Spots of color appeared on the traveler's otherwise-pale face. "Sir, the dog has been inside the transport three times now. I obviously have nothing to hide."

A second agent, Hansen, stepped forward. "You wrote *Household Goods* on your declaration form," he said, looking up from the document. "Value: 200 dollars, US funds. Is that right?"

The old man sighed and nodded.

"What about this desk?" Thomas leaned into the van and lifted the corner of a packing blanket to reveal the desk's foot, carved in dark wood.

"It's a piece of junk. Yard sale stuff." The traveler grunted as he climbed inside and unbuckled the packing strap that held the desk to the wall. He shook his head slowly and glanced at his watch as he pulled the padding off and gingerly stepped down from the van.

Flashlight in hand, Hansen climbed in. He squatted above a rusty lawn mower parked next to a faded 70s RadarRange with a price tag: *$10 or best offer*. He twisted the flashlight and played an LED beam between two columns of drawers into an empty kneehole recess. The beam illuminated a yellowed paper label on the underside of the desk: *John Townsend, Newport*. One by one, he removed the drawers and aimed the beam inside. Straightening up, he looked to the driver outside in the holding area. "This desk is worth more than the 200 dollars you declared as the value of all your cargo, Mr. Smith."

"Why?" the driver protested. He reached in and ran his hand over the peeling surface. "It needs to be refinished. Can't you see? Change my estimate to 400 if you want. I don't care." He looked at his watch again.

Hansen looked deeper into the cargo in the van. He turned to the driver, bathed in the sodium glow. "What's in the crate behind that box of Christmas lights?"

Smith seemed to lose more of the little color he had and said, "It's a painting. Fragile. Can't you see the frame?"

"Take it out, please. We're trained to be careful."

"I'll need a screwdriver. I must protest. I make this crossing twice a month. This is outrageous."

Thomas handed Smith a Makita power drill. Smith backed out five screws and pulled off the lid. The agent lifted a painting of a gentleman from the box.

"Frame's the only value here," Smith said. "They call these portraits *instant relatives* at the auction houses around here."

"Nice crating for a worthless painting, Mr. Smith," Hansen said. He examined the old oil for an artist's signature or inscription on the back but found none.

"I'm a careful packer," Smith said, "Call it a curse."

"What's under the tarp?"

"A ratty old table. See for yourself."

Hansen looked over his shoulder at the driver wilting under the inspection lights and lifted the tarp. A long, old drop leaf table stood on simple dark mahogany legs.

"It's just a plain table," Smith shouted. "No carving at all. A loser."

The flashlight revealed another Townsend label on the underside. "Where'd you say you found this load, Mr. Smith?" he asked, climbing out into the light.

"A yard sale up in Sooke, on the coast."

"Do you have a receipt, a sales slip? Something that identifies these items?"

"It was a yard sale. They don't give receipts. Why are you doing this to me?"

"I'm protecting the security of my homeland, sir. Why are you protesting so much?"

"I have to get to Tacoma by five or the auction house closes for the weekend and I'll waste two evenings in some fleabag motel till they open on Monday."

"What auction house?"

"Ah ... Brown's Auction."

"I think I went to one of their sales. Over by the old Pantages Theater. That fella, Brown, is quite a character, isn't he?"

"I've heard. I never met the man."

"Mr. Smith, I'm a bit of an antique lover myself and that's a nice old desk, refinished or not. Chippendale style, I'd say," he said, watching the old man try to evade the inspector's eyes.

"It's in the Chippendale style, as you call it," Smith said. "I can see there's no fooling an expert. I was just guessing low on the price. You never know what will happen at an auction."

"I'm going to ask you to increase the value of your household goods by 500 dollars, Mr. Smith."

Smith shrugged.

"Do you ever find Mission oak pieces?"

"All the time," Smith said, as he tightened the furniture strap, his back to the agent.

"A guy comes around here, a nut for Stickley. Has the balls to come to the Homeland Security office here and ask us to notify him if we spot a piece of it as we inspect the vehicles entering the US. Even left a poster for the office. He asked me to hand out his cards to anyone we thought would do him good. I have one in my pocket. Want one?" A card with a picture of a Morris chair and a phone number said, *Mission Oak Wanted*.

Smith accepted the card, crumpled it and threw the wad into the heap of stuff in his van. "I have plenty of people to sell Stickley to," he said.

"Bring the dog back," Hansen said and frowned. Smith sagged. "Just kidding, Mr. Smith. A little homeland security humor ... gotcha, didn't I?"

Smith's face wrinkled; confusion, maybe, or relief.

6

"You're right about the auctions, I've been to a few, as I said. Go on now. Tacoma's two hours away, but mark my words. That desk is worth more than you think. In the right auction you might be surprised."

"The guy in the red van, he was a squirrel," the dog handler said. His wet boots left a puddle of Pacific Northwest moisture on the government-gray desk as he leaned back in the office chair.

"I pegged him as a bottom feeder who scored some quality pieces at a yard sale and was hustling down to a real auction house to see how he did," Hansen said. "Slipped him one of Wally Winchester's cards but he threw it away, the old fart. There goes our chance to make fifty bucks."

He looked at the poster. Hand drawn at their office a month before, to the amusement of the office staff, it hung above the door, next to framed federal documents. A photo of that wall had been a hit on government employee e-mail threads. Above a sketch of a Mission table and chair, the sign read: *$50 Reward for tips that lead to my purchase of Stickley Company Mission oak antique furniture.* A contact phone number for Wally Winchester, Camano Island, USA was scrawled across the bottom.

The sign on the wall had been the subject of two minor reprimands from the regional office. "Sorry, Wally," he said to the poster and grinned. "I think I let one get away."

Chapter One

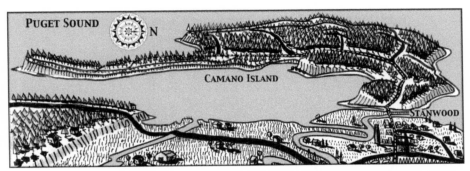

Camano Island, Washington

The phone call came at 10 PM.

"What's the most valuable piece of American furniture ever sold?" It was a snarl familiar to Wally Winchester.

Sitting alone in his cabin on the edge of a hundred-foot drop with Puget Sound below, he looked down at the phone. The display read *UNAVAILABLE*. Across the room, a vintage 70s RCA television showed the Mariners ahead six to two in the ninth. Wally was watching the game, swirling red wine in a glass. "Is this you, Brown?"

"Never mind. Answer the question. The best ever found?"

"Ed ...? Oh, all right. Probably that hairy paw Chippendale arm chair from Philadelphia."

"Nice try. Think Rhode Island."

It was Ed, he concluded, Ed Brown, an old picking partner from Tacoma, now an auctioneer. He sat up, lifting stocking feet off the Machine Age aluminum coffee table in front of him, careful not to scratch the original Formica top. Leaning back against the 50s version of a Frank Lloyd Wright sectional sofa, his favorite seat in the cabin, he ran his fingers through a thick mop of unruly dirty-blond hair turning gray at his ears. He rubbed his stubbly chin and said, "How about a Goddard and Townsend block-front secretary?"

"Very good, Wally-boy, and I thought you were just a Stickley whore."

"I grew up in New England where everyone knew something about 18th century things. What you get?"

"An interesting item for an auction."

"You son of a bitch! *You* got a piece of period Rhode Island furniture? That could be worth millions! How the hell did you get your hands on something that important way out here?"

"Five million, in fact," Ed said, "and I hope you washed your hands today." Ed had a thing about dirty hands.

It was an old joke, a product of many days on the road together, side-by-side in a U-Haul rental box, headed for the giant flea markets in the Northeast, as they tried to root out old things on antiquing trips across America.

"It came to me, actually," Brown continued. "I was taking a nap in the apartment above the shop and Laura woke me to tell me about this consignor who'd walked in off the street with a plan to sell off a long-lost collection of Rhode Island Chippendale. Made Newport by the greatest cabinetmaker of the 18th century, purchased by a local doctor, got sent to Canada in 1765, and dropped out of sight. Last week, 230 years later, the collection was a hundred miles north of my auction house, on Vancouver Island—still owned by the same family, passed down from first-born son to first-born son. You know these family heirlooms."

"I got it," said Wally.

Ed wasn't finished. "Provenance and everything! There's even an oil painting of the original owner, the doctor, a guy named Moffatt."

"Holy shit. How much do *you* get?"

"There's a complicated sliding scale on the commission. It's a tiny percentage, actually. Based on the sale price. There's too much competition for something this important."

"Yeah, I bet." Wally had read about the price wars back East among the mammoth auction houses for the right to handle the sale of blue-chip estates, like Princess Margaret's jewels. With 40 or 50 million dollars at stake, auction houses were willing to pay a number *higher* than the hammer price to an important consignor, thanks to the....

"Buyer's premium," Ed said quietly.

"Oh my God, the buyer's premium!" Wally said, pondering percentages. "How much is your second sticker, you thief?"

"Ten percent over hammer price."

Wally did the math and blurted into the phone, "You're going to make 500,000 dollars for five minutes work! You bastard!"

"You can see me do this auction this Saturday, but it'll cost you 50 bucks to get in."

"You must be kidding. You want me to pay you 50 dollars to watch you make half a million dollars in five minutes?" Wally was both amused and outraged.

"Yup. There are only five people in the world who will be players in this sale, and none of them lives closer than 3,000 miles away. I don't want anyone in the room except for those five guys and the media. This is a high-class event. Laura's going all out with finger food for the gods. Fifty big ones will keep the riffraff out. The only people I want to see there are guys with five million to spend or press passes."

"Even me, your old traveling buddy, you son-of-a-bitch, after all we've been through together?"

"Especially you."

11

Chapter Two

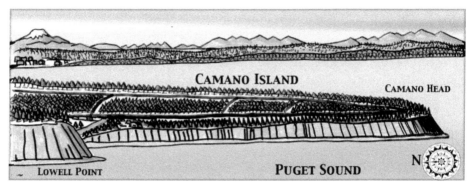

Camano Island, Washington

Two cups of coffee into the morning, Wally was on the phone.

"*Maine Antique Digest*. This is Sam." The editor, himself. Wally knew his byline. It was amazing that Sam answered the phone.

"Did you folks hear about the Chippendale furniture up for auction out here this Saturday?" Wally asked.

"You calling from the Pacific Northwest, son?"

"Yes sir, I'm going to attend the Moffatt estate sale down in Tacoma and thought I could write up a report for your paper. This collection was made by—"

"We know the Moffatt story … what did you say your name is?"

"Wally, Walter Winchester."

"We're sending one of our reporters to the auction, Wally. Sorry. Thanks for calling."

"I can save your magazine the plane fare if you like. I'm 20 years in the business, and I'll be there."

"Our guy cut his teeth on Newport furniture, coauthored a book about it. You?"

Strike one.

He poured another pot full of water into a chrome-bottomed Bunn-o-Matic and watched the instant action of hot water on free-trade grounds. He caught the first offerings in his cup.

The pile of glossy antique magazines on a table next to the phone offered another option. Wally opened the most recent issue to the Publisher Directory on page three, and searched for the editorial office phone number. None was listed. Undaunted, he dialed the main number to find a way in. After five minutes of fast talking, he reached the executive editor.

"Rachel speaking."

"Hello, my name is Walter Winchester and I want to write an article for your magazine."

"How did you get this number?"

"*Er* ... I found it in the February issue, the one with the Matthew Prior painting on the cover."

"My number isn't listed there."

"Yes, I found that out. The operator sent me to you."

"They don't do that here without a name or extension. I'm going to hang up now."

"Wait. OK, Rachel, I called the advertising department, that call went right through. Chatted up someone named Maurice about a full-page ad, asked him about the quality of the editorial staff. He mentioned you. Said you're a publishing legend. Then I surfed the directory and called you."

"You worked pretty hard to get here. You have 30 seconds and then I hang up."

"OK, there's an auction out here in the Northwest next Saturday. A legendary set of Chippendale items just came to light. Estimated value, five million plus. I want to cover the sale for you."

"What have you written? Have I seen anything you've done?"

"Actually, I haven't had anything in print for 20 years."

Click.

Strike two. Wally shook it off and stepped back into the batter's box.

"Rachel, Wally again. I'm a real good writer, you'll see. This sale could be a major event in the auction year. I'm already going there. Let me do a piece for you."

A phone noise signaled Rachel, in real time, cutting into her voicemail. "I refuse to hire a person unknown to me, Mr. Winchester, but if you write something up after the sale I promise you I'll look at it. Don't call me again."

Home run, Wally thought. Time to make that press pass.

Wally adjusted the Photoshopped *PRESS PASS* card pinned to his shirt. The auction was scheduled to begin at 10 AM, which had meant leaving Camano Island at the crack of dawn with a notebook, a checkbook, a portable tape recorder, and his trusty old Nikon.

Early morning sunshine backlit the Cascade Mountains as Wally's Blue Dodge van passed 10 acres of bulldozed soil to the right of the freeway. A wise old glass dealer once lived where a construction shack now stood, one of his automatic right turns on a picking route south. Always had a new lot of art glass shades when he stopped. Always asked too much. Word in the trade, she sold her shop and three acres off the freeway access road for 500,000 dollars to make room for a Home Depot parking lot. *There's that half-million number again. Everybody's making money but me.* Wally shook his head as he weaved in and out of light commuter traffic.

Bungalow-studded hillsides of the old port town of Everett loomed above a lingering fogbank pierced by construction cranes and ship masts. Hewitt Avenue, a canyon of four story brick storefronts from the good old days, flashed by on the passenger side. Wally had made a big hit on a street like that, many years before and 3,000 miles away. He'd often brag about his score during the long road trips to the Midwest with Brown in the U-Haul, crashing local farm auctions, beating out prairie doorknockers and pickers to buy antiques at half their worth. Brown always tried to top him with a story of his own.

Seattle disappeared under an ivy-covered concrete slab spanning the interstate. *Half a million dollars.* Wally eased the old Dodge into the center lane away from the clogged exits under the tunnel. *Now it's Brown's turn to gloat, the rat bastard.*

The usual sandwich board signs advertising Brown's auctions to the public weren't there. Wally parked on a nearly deserted street in front of Brown's building on Broadway's Antique Row. The West Coast hadn't been invited. A sign on the door said: *CLOSED TODAY. PRIVATE AUCTION.* He felt like a thief as he flashed his press pass at the teenager hired to guard the door. Wally walked by him without paying. *Fuck you and your fifty dollars, Ed.* On his way to the auction floor, he walked through a selection of European chandeliers and showcases filled with oddities.

Across a sea of empty chairs, three objects were visible on the stage: a desk, a table, and an ornately framed painting.

The Browns stood near a table displaying a pitcher of fresh-squeezed orange juice, baby chocolate éclairs, today's shrimp, fresh

Dungeness crab, Samish Island oysters on the half shell, and Tulalip Indian smoked salmon with capers. Ed, wearing a black turtleneck under a well-cut sport coat over tan chinos, was chatting across the table with a TV news reporter. His wife, Laura, beside him, wore a designer suit. Her long red Shirley Temple curls seemed to have a life of their own. Her earrings and necklace looked like Lalique to Wally.

He saw others, bona fide members of the legitimate press.

A photographer fiddled with the fat lens on his Nikon while standing next to a fellow wearing a *Tacoma News Tribune* press pass. Wally figured him as a reporter. Two video people from Seattle TV stations were installing a long microphone cable. Another reporter, wearing a *Seattle Times* nametag, huddled over his cell phone.

The people at the food table were also strangers.

A salt-and-pepper haired, bearded gentleman wearing L. L. Bean clothes nibbled on a shrimp. Wally pegged him as the reporter from the *Maine Antique Digest,* a long way from home.

Backed against the wall, sipping coffee, an older fellow wore a pained look on his gaunt, gray face. Wally guessed, consignor.

The third figure was working the chocolate éclair display, three mini-confections on a delicate china plate. A large drooping brown moustache punctuated a jovial "trust me" face. Wally did. *Antique dealer, probably high-end period items, judging from the professional polish of his smile.*

The fourth man at the table stood erect, but relaxed, a casual, but watchful, approximation of parade rest. He nursed a glass of juice. A curlicue of dark hair fell over his broad forehead; his face was angular and weather-wrinkled. Wally, startled, flashed on the face of John Kerry in the presidential election watching the state of Florida slip away. Sadness etched lines under the man's eyes. *It's not Kerry, not in that suit. An unknown character who might be a genius software millionaire, or an aging musician with a big bank account. Or a deadbeat who managed to get in.* Wally struck that last thought, reasoning Brown wouldn't have let a street person this close to his thousand-dollar snacks. He couldn't figure the man's place in the strangely assembled group, here to witness a five million dollar, five minute auction. He wasn't part of the press crowd.

Piling six shrimp and two éclairs onto a china plate, he introduced himself to the stranger. "Hello I'm Walter Winchester. Are you into computers? You look familiar."

"My name is Ivanchenko." The accent sounded as Russian as the name.

"You here to buy the desk, Mr. Chenko?" Wally decided he shouldn't offer his hand while he held an empty shrimp tail in his fingers.

"Ivanchenko. Yvgeney Ivanchenko. Yvgeney is my given name."

"Interested in the desk, Geney?"

"Yv-geney. *YV* is the first part. *Geney* rhymes with penny. *Yvgeney.* To answer your question, I have no intention of a purchase. I am a visitor, a tourist to this place. I was invited to attend this sale by the man, Brown, standing there." Wally had known private collectors with big checkbooks who told better stories.

"Are you in the business?"

"I do not understand the question. If you can tell me what *the business* is, I will tell you if I am in it." His eyes locked on Wally's. Both men waited for a blink, but neither got one.

"Antique dealer, conservator, buying agent, collector."

"If those are the businesses you ask me if I am in, the answer is no."

"Big fan of Chippendale?" Wally said, looking for an exit.

"Chippendale is an ornamental style, popular in the English colonies and in Great Britain in the mid-to-late 18th century. While I appreciate the value of it as decorative art, I cannot say that I am a fan. I am a fan of *The Simpsons*. I have heard many episodes."

"Excuse me." He gave the odd Russian tourist the gate and turned to big moustache. "Here to take home the desk? Walter Winchester," this time extending his hand, squeezing a meaty paw.

"Dieter Holtzman. The desk? Nah, I couldn't afford it. What are they expecting it to bring? Five million? Heck, I was just out here camping, got wind of the sale and decided to check it out. What do you think of it?"

Wally knew that no sane person went camping in the North Cascades in March, but he kept talking. "Haven't gone up to see it yet. The food looked too good." Wally said, remembering the snow level in the Cascades. *Snow on the summit all the way down to a thousand feet elevation. Hard March rain every day this week till this morning. Nice time to pitch a tent.* "You in the business?"

A smile lifted both corners of the moustache. He said, "I dabble in antiques. Buy and sell a little. I have a little store in Maine. The desk's a fake, no doubt about it. If it goes cheap it would be nice to have as a study piece. If you're an expert … Walter, I'd love to hear your thoughts."

"Actually, my specialty is 20th century, back to Stickley. Don't think my opinion would help you make a decision."

"You might be surprised. Tell me what you think." He paused. "Why are you here, Walter?"

"Ed wanted a witness."

Plucking another glass of juice, Wally saluted Brown, then turned toward the white-bearded consignor standing against the wall, and watched him retreat.

Gotta be the consignor, guy's in a pickle if the desk turns out to be wrong. He moved toward Brown and his wife, deep in conversation with one of the reporters, but turned to the stage instead. Two strides forward, Wally turned around to check out the people in the hall. No one new had arrived. *No one's here to pay five million for the desk. No big shots. No New York bidders.*

Five minutes to 10. The auction was about to begin. He turned his attention to the objects for sale.

All three sale items carried hastily scribbled disclaimers propped up on folded pieces of cardboard. The desk was not a form well known to Wally, but his untrained eye deemed it magnificent. It was a writing desk with a flat top and matching columns of drawers with block-carved fronts. The long top drawer sported three carved shells—two proud of the surface, the middle one recessed. Flat brass hardware fit the period. Boldly dovetailed, carved bracket feet gave it a sense of stability. A badly peeling varnish layer appeared old but not original, a reasonable condition for furniture 245 years old. Under the top was a hard-to-read paper label:

MADE BY
JOHN TOWNSEND
NEWPORT
RHODE ISLAND

It had been lacquered over. A shiny coating over a paper label is a bad sign. It stopps further inspection of the age of the paper. He looked at furniture maker's marks every time he entered a shop. Tilting tables was part of the trade. The brasses, dovetails, and carving appeared to be well crafted, as one would expect from America's premier cabinetmaker. Wally had never seen a Newport shell-carved desk up so close before. There was no way for him, a turn-of-the-century Stickley buyer, to draw any conclusions about its authenticity.

He didn't care. He wasn't here to buy it. He was there as a reporter and a reluctant bystander to his friend's potential windfall. The millionaire dealers and their experts would vote on the fine details with their checkbooks. Those people who were still absent as the auction time neared in the curiously vacant hall.

The cardboard sign sitting on the desk explained the empty room:

THIS DESK IS <u>NOT</u> AN ANTIQUE

Beside the desk on the stage, a drop-leaf table sporting single-board sides stood long and narrow on the oriental carpet. The finish was rich mahogany brown, polished a thousand times. The legs were flat-sided Chippendale columns with vertical grooves that met the top at a simple skirt. A lacquered paper label under this one, similarly indistinct, identified the maker as John Townsend. A cardboard sign placed on top said:

This is an authentic table, circa 1765.
The label appears to have been added.

The third lot was a medium-sized oil portrait of a man in an old, but conservative, frame. The sitter's clothing said 18th century. The cardboard sign said:

Painting, circa 1765.

Original Finish

Not necessarily Dr. Thomas Moffatt

The auction was scheduled to begin in two minutes, but there were no signs of buyers with five million to spend. Wally returned to the food table, helping himself to another large glass of juice and a sample of the Tulalip salmon. *Where are the bidders?*

Brown, glaring at Wally's press pass, walked slowly toward the stage, darting his eyes over the nearly empty hall, darkening further as his old road partner helped himself to another three-dollar tumbler of juice as if it were a wedding toast, tossing it down in a gulp like a shot of rye.

"My name is Ed Brown," he began. "I have been commissioned to offer for sale the following three objects: The first is a portrait, perhaps of Dr. Thomas Moffatt, circa 1760. The second being the Thomas Moffatt Newport drop-leaf table with John Townsend label. The third being the Thomas Moffatt Newport kneehole three shell desk with John Townsend label."

"We'll begin the bidding with the portrait of Dr. Thomas Moffatt, circa 1760."

Wally sat in a nearly empty room, on a Saturday morning where five million dollars worth of furniture was about to be auctioned off to an audience which consisted of the auctioneer's wife, the consignor, two camera operators, two newspaper reporters, one magazine reporter from Maine, a local television news reporter, a photographer, a clueless Russian tourist, a dealer and camper from Maine, and himself, pretending to be a writer because he didn't want to pay the 50 dollar gate fee.

Wally thought Brown looked like a professional golfer, with crisply creased tan trousers over shiny shoes as he stood before the microphone. By Pacific Northwest standards, he looked sharp. His handsome European features and naturally well-developed body had always seemed unfair. Wally had felt like the chubby one in the background on their picking trips.

"We're going to start the bidding at 3,000 dollars," Brown said, his strong voice echoing.

No answer.

"Do we have 2,000 for this portrait?"

Silence.

"A thousand dollars we have."

Wally quickly looked around. Had somebody come in? Did that dealer from Maine bid? Wally doubted it. Oil paintings of unknown instant relatives, even old ones, are difficult to sell unless the artist was famous or an important naïve painter.

The bidder was the consigner, Smith.

"Sold. For 1,000 dollars to ... number ..." Smith defiantly held up his card. "Bidder number 1-2-5." The auctioneer sneered theatrically at the bidder before turning his attention to the remaining objects.

How bizarre, Wally thought, the consignor's buying his own stuff back.

"Item number two is the Thomas Moffatt Newport drop-leaf table. I'd like to see 3,000." No response. "Do we have 2,000?" The question was more like a statement, a taunt to an empty room.

Wally was having a revelation. Other than the make-believe camper, he was the only antique dealer in a five million dollar, no reserve auction.

"One hundred dollars." Wally said, to lowball Brown for the Chippendale table.

"One hundred dollars is bid." Brown sounded poisonous. Wally, the only person in the room in a position to *buy* this table, smiled back pleasantly. Brown scowled from the podium as Wally, munching a baby éclair, held up his paddle. The auctioneer, no stranger to bouncing his own bids against the wall, had no one in the room to blame for a phantom bid except reporters and a Russian tourist. Wally, invited to witness Brown's triumph, was enjoying this way too much.

"Do we have 200?" The auctioneer plaintively asked the empty chairs. Wally just grinned.

"Two hundred."

Wally spun around. The bidder was the cameraman from *Channel Seven News,* caught up in the strange empty circus.

That's OK, Wally reasoned.

"Two hundred I have. Do I see 300?"

Wally turned to the cameraman, stared him down while raising the paddle higher, watching the upstart fold and lower his hand. The gavel cracked. Wally had just paid for his trip to Tacoma.

"Sold ... to number 1-1-7. Damn it!" Brown said, glaring at Wally more venomously than before.

This was a rare moment. Wally, knowing that few people who shook hands with Ed Brown got all their fingers back, was thinking that it was a very good morning, indeed.

Two gallery assistants came on stage as if on cue. They carefully lifted the Chippendale desk and placed it on a flat dolly. Brown took a gallon can of gasoline from behind the podium. Moving carefully, the assistants rolled the fancy desk off the stage, across the auction floor toward the sidewalk, followed by the press and everyone else.

Brown walked over behind the desk, its peeling finish glistening in the unusual Tacoma sunshine. He stretched taller than his five-foot-eleven frame, holding the can of gas. "Because of the controversy and deception swirling around this larcenous attempt to defraud the antiques community at large and, in particular, my business and major clients on the East Coast—"

Brown delivered his little sermon / monologue in a theatrical try for moral outrage. Staring directly at the consignor, Brown's voice rose in majestic indignation. "I have decided to withdraw from this sale the John Townsend Newport three shell American Chippendale desk!"

Shaking and fuming, he continued his tirade, still aiming his wrath squarely at the wilting consignor. "You, sir, have an opportunity to erase the perfidy of your deeds! I suggest you do the right thing to avoid prosecution and guarantee that this … egregious fraud, this black stain on the reputations of honest antique dealers … will never again resurface to deceive future innocents. I command you to put it to sleep forever." Like a preacher chastising a sinner, Brown handed Smith the gas can.

Brown called the Tacoma police, commanding them to take the desk away as evidence. The bemused cops said, "No thanks, we don't take furniture in as evidence. Whaddaya think we look like—movers?" They drove away, laughing.

As the *Maine Antique Digest* reported it later, Brown had been wavering between canceling the sale altogether or simply announcing that the kneehole's authenticity was in serious doubt. The article did note that the auctioneer was notorious for his offbeat antics and outrageous stunts, thriving on controversy. "My integrity was on the line," Brown told the reporter. "I toyed with the idea of setting the desk on fire in front of the reporters and TV cameras as a way to save face, but I knew it wasn't a good plan. In the lawsuit that would surely follow, the only evidence would be ashes. The lack of interest by the major buyers and collectors would be a lousy defense at a million-dollar trial."

Wally was whistling 10 minutes later as he lifted the period Chippendale table—fake label or not—into his van. By his calculations, he had just made 2,000 dollars. The consignor, of course, had not set his desk on fire.

"This story," Wally said aloud, "might be worth writing after all."

Standing in a shadowy doorway near the auction house, the Russian squinted into bright noonday sun he assumed uncommon for April in the Pacific Northwest. The light flooded the dampened asphalt of Tacoma's Antique Row. He spoke into a small tape recorder as he watched the shaggy-haired antique dealer lift the drop-leaf table into a van and wrap it with a blanket.

Dusky smoke clouded the pavement behind the transport as the badly-tuned engine cleared its throat and roared to life. The object of his interest was about to leave Tacoma, destination unknown. The Russian reached for his keys.

Chapter Three

Interstate Route Five, Marysville, Washington

The temperature gauge on the dusty dashboard warned that the coolant was about to boil over again. Wally frowned, calculating the distance to the Marysville exit so he could throw in some water, which he figured would be good for the last 30 miles. Considering the valuable cargo, a vintage Chippendale table, and the fun he'd had beating Brown at his own game while scarfing down about a hundred dollars worth of exotic finger food, he decided to play it safe and top off the radiator before continuing north to Camano Island. What a bizarre auction, he thought, turning the heater on full and opening the driver's window to suck out the hot air stream at his feet. *I was the only one in the room who made any money today.* The dial on the temperature gauge slowly moved back into view, stopping shy of 220 degrees as the Marysville exit sign appeared. He drove on by, turning off the blinker, secure in the knowledge that nothing could go wrong today. He was on a roll. And he was looking forward to reporting it all to *Art and Antiques Magazine.*

The exit to Camano Island was number 212. FM radio blasting Saturday afternoon rhythm & blues, Wally failed to notice the rented mid-sized Ford sedan that had followed him at a distance ever since he left Tacoma.

At the end of the off-ramp he turned left and drove under the highway toward the town of Stanwood. The bridge to Camano Island was five miles west. After the bridge, he had 15 more miles of island driving before he reached his cabin on the southwest tip, but it was mileage he enjoyed. Wally flipped the window visor down for the expected late afternoon sun and knew that he was home.

Vast panoramas flickered by between the tall, second-growth firs, summer cottages, and newly developed properties. The massive spine of the Cascade Mountains formed the jagged eastern horizon to the left.

His driveway was a dirt road to the right at milepost 18. It meandered from West Camano Drive through a grove of cedars down to the western edge of the island. The orange mirror of Puget Sound and the snow-covered peaks of the Olympics came into view as his old blue Dodge van shuddered over potholes and the shiny tops of cedar roots. Wally parked next to his cabin. Steam from the radiator billowed from the grill. He scratched a note to himself to put water in it and stuck it on the steering wheel where he couldn't miss it the next day. An eagle flying over the precipice caught his eye. He waved.

Wally didn't notice the black Ford sedan behind him on the road above. It slowed and pulled over as it passed the driveway.

The ramshackle studio cabin sat 50 feet back from a high bank above the beach. On the weathered green front door, a vintage gold-lettered courthouse sign announced *Harry Studley, Deputy Sheriff.* Wally entered, noticing that most of his antique lamps had been left on earlier. They glowed weakly, overpowered by the sunset flooding the front window. He smiled. He liked old lights.

Visitors to his cabin most often commented on the lighting. Odd mechanical and electrical devices were screwed into, or otherwise protruded, from every wall. Some lamps with green glass shades hung from accordion-like iron fixtures similar to the old candlestick phones used by police dispatchers in black-and-white films. Walking over to one of his prize possessions, a Limbert Company quarter-sawn oak table, he glanced at the voicemail recorder, noted five new messages and uncorked a Washington red from a Yakima vineyard. The sunset behind glacier-clad peaks faded from deep orange to a backlit purple before his eyes. He waved at that also, thanking whoever was responsible for that moment, and sat back. He was home.

Wally's shoulders, stiff from the three-hour return trip, relaxed as he surveyed his domain. Framed paintings, prints, and vintage-framed, sepia-foxed broadsheets plastered the walls. A portrait of Albert Einstein by the Canadian photographer, Karsh, hung beside the foam-covered bench that Wally used as a bed. Two Oriental rugs hung like towels from a pair of ornate white-painted picture frames picked up on an earlier trip to Victoria. Four Navajo blankets, including one for a chief, were folded and draped on a small oak settee with side spindles. Through the front window, he watched lazy wisps of steam leaking from under the cover of the cedar-sided hot tub that sat near the edge of the bank. Wally debated calling his girlfriend and inviting her over for a soak, but figured he should begin writing his magazine article while the events of the bizarre auction were fresh in his mind. Turning on the portable tape recorder, he heard a tinny version of Brown's voice berating the consignor. He fired up his G4 computer, found a word program, and began to type.

The last of sunset faded behind the distant mountain range. The rambling American Craftsman lodge was expensive, promising a gourmet breakfast and Internet access. The Russian did not notice the view. He stared at the screen of his laptop.

"Walter Winchester of Camano Island, Washington, has no criminal record except a 22-year-old charge of indecent exposure at a football field while he was in college. The auctioneer, Ed Brown, from Tacoma has numerous convictions for selling stolen goods, including one in which he was found guilty of selling the contents of the wrong hotel. Nothing suggests he is capable of masterminding a major crime. He has made numerous trips to Europe since the 90s. Seven times to Germany last year. He imports antiques. No European warrants. The name, Smith, from Vancouver Island, Canada, was impossible to narrow down, as you might imagine. The firm of Goddard and Townsend from Newport, Rhode Island, did indeed create important furniture in the American Chippendale style. Some of the most expensive American furniture ever sold. A high chest-on-frame realized six million dollars two years ago at a major auction in New York."

Satisfied with the response, he pulled a dark wool watch cap over his light brown hair and left the fancy inn for a look at the cabin where the dealer lived.

Chapter Four

Camano Island, Washington

"I'm leaving for Vancouver Island," Wally said to Rae Roberts, his current love. Her tall body was backlit by the last of the sunset as she sat on the side of his hot tub. Blonde hair framed a Nordic face. "Gonna write an article for a magazine. Gotta find a guy named Smith for an interview. Wanna come along?"

Rae slipped back into the hot water, joining Wally and Lucy Adams, a neighbor.

"I can't, Wally," she said, the water now up to her chin. "I have photo shoots all week, and a wedding on Sunday."

"We'll be back way before Sunday, babe. Is there any way you can reschedule the sittings? Think about all the fun we could have, a couple of ferry rides, great dinners at waterfront cafes, days on the road to explore. Don't make that face." He splashed her. "And don't forget, sweetie," he moved closer and draped an arm over her shoulders. "Romantic nights in exotic locales."

"The last exotic locale I slept in with you gave me a rash. I looked like a pincushion for two weeks. I will always remember Victor's Rustic Cabins."

"Sorry about that one, Rae. Old Victor hasn't kept the place up these last years. How old do you think he is, 80? Do you realize how rare it is to find a hundred-year-old fishing camp with the original furniture still intact? I want to stay close to the old codger. In case he calls it quits."

"You took me to that vermin-infested auto court because you wanted to swindle an old man out of his log furniture? You told me it would be a vacation in an art hotel."

Wally smiled. "Don't you think it was worth a few flea bites to sleep in that great folk-art bed?"

Rae laughed back. "That headboard had so many branches I was afraid we were being attacked by powder post beetles."

"Do you know how much that bed would bring in a Christie's sale?"

"Then I thought, termites. Wood-eating, flying ants. When the bites began I figured they had turned on humans."

"Twelve thousand. Minimum. He has six cabins. Do the math."

"Later, as you snored, I thought about flesh-eating bacteria. Did you see the filth in that old man's kitchen? I'm surprised he's lived as long as he has."

Wally moved on, "Hey, Snookums, we could renew our vows."

"We haven't declared any vows," she answered, disengaging his arm. She slid to a neutral corner of the tub.

"Not yet. Do you remember that time we stepped out a heart in the sand around my friends, Harry and Cecilia? Up on Tofino beach? They got married a month later."

"She was pregnant."

31

"Good timing, then, that we got them to fall in love. Vancouver Island is a magical place, Rae. Take a chance and go on an adventure with me. You never know what to expect up there."

"I really can't reschedule, Wally. Sorry. Take Lucy, she doesn't have a life."

The woman beside her splashed water in Rae's face with a sweep of her hand and turned to Wally. "You know I'm always up for adventure, sweetheart," Lucy said in a Liverpool twang as she rose, silhouetted by the sunset, from the submerged seat. She adjusted a cap that kept her dark hair from the damp and pulled her full lips into a pout aimed at Rae. "I love my life, thank you," she said, batting her deep-set brown eyes at Wally. "But I am free for a couple days this week if you want the company. You know the rules—separate beds. That all right with you, Rae?"

"Separate beds is a good rule. Wally, don't forget," Rae said, as she looked at Lucy.

Chapter Five

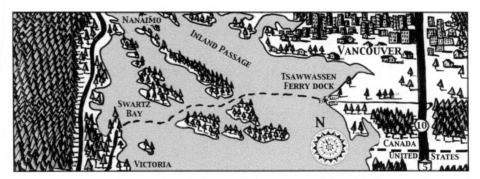

Queen of Sannich Ferry, Upper Puget Sound

The journey from Camano to Vancouver Island was a 60-mile drive north to the Canadian border, a 29-mile left turn out to a ferry terminal, a two-hour boat ride through the northern San Juan Islands, and a minor confrontation over Lucy's British passport.

"I love the *Queen of Sannich* ferry run. It slows me right down. Did you ever see that pet food commercial that claimed owning a cat can lower your blood pressure?" Wally said.

Lucy said she didn't watch TV.

"This boat ride always does it for me," Wally said, sitting on a padded bench in the upper passenger lounge of the car ferry as it threaded its way through the narrow, tide-churned waterway between rugged islands off the coast of British Columbia.

Wally surveyed the gaggle of travelers surrounding them in the spacious passenger lounge. A wall of upturned *Vancouver Sun* front pages hid a number of faces.

"Lucy," Wally said. "Behind you. Three fluffy-haired gals, over by the window. What's their story, do you think?"

Lucy turned her head, arcing past a pair of pregnant Northwest aboriginal women, chatting in a strange dialect. Past a young logger and his girlfriend, who, oblivious to the scenery outside the large windows, were kissing. A group of scruffy, about-14-year-old-skinhead hoodlums filled the tiny arcade.

The vessel shuddered perceptibly, changing course between the two surprisingly close rocky shorelines. Three deer grazed in a sunny clearing to the left, suggesting that the cliff-side home beside them was not inhabited. Another ferry dock, too modest for their vessel, appeared. Lucy gestured at the craggy land. "This is my TV," she said. "Mother Nature."

"My point exactly," Wally said. "There's nothing more calming to me than the British Columbia Ferry Service taking the steering wheel from my hands and saying, Relax ... there's nothing for you to do for the next two hours ... read the paper ... look for orcas ... have a bowl of chowder ... gather your thoughts ... gawk at the interesting people. Whaddya say we go outside, Lucy? Sit on the deck and get some sun."

Wally opened the outside door for Lucy. Cool spring air whipped at their faces.

"Did they have ferries like this back East when you were living there?" asked Lucy, searching the waves for orca fins.

Wally didn't answer right away. He was remembering a much earlier passage: "A few years back, maybe 20 now, I took a big boat to Martha's Vineyard, off the coast of Massachusetts. It ran between Cape Cod and the island. I went there to get away from the antique business."

"I thought you love the antique business, Wally. Ever since I've known you you've been consumed by it." The wind nearly took her words.

"Not that day. Seven days in a row, sleeping under a truck at the Brimfield Flea Market—the summer show, the hot one—was in my head. Martha's Vineyard was the closest thing to a desert island I could find. Besides, I had an invitation."

"A chiquita?"

"Actually, it was a creativity class, a U-Mass course."

"You? You're an antique dealer. What was the class, *Creativity 701, Swindling Old Ladies Outside the Box?*"

"I buy mostly from other antique dealers, and they deserve to be swindled. No, it was *Problem Solving 101.* It was a serious group. Rodney Dangerfield was in our class, but we never saw him. He took the course over the phone."

"Can you speak up?" She had to shout over the wind gusts.

Wally steered her to the lee of a bulkhead. Another shudder rocked the deck as the ferry exited the close island passage, turning right into a vast bay. "I took the class for grins, maybe give me an edge over the cutthroat sons-of-bitches I deal with. I learned a lot. The weekend retreat to Martha's Vineyard for the last class was the professor's idea. He owned a gingerbread house in Oak Bluff, a restored Victorian village on the west shore of the island."

Lucy nodded.

"The island appealed to me because I was sick and tired of antiques. Seven days at Brimfield, looking into the backs of thousands of trucks at 5 AM, flashlight in hand, making terrifying decisions involving lots of money with three people behind me maybe ready to buy, and if I hesitated, they'd laugh later about that idiot in front of them who passed on it. Was the chair really a Frank Lloyd Wright design? Was it really old?"

Lucy watched him, attentive.

"Then there were the mornings, wired tight on coffee, fast-walking through endless mazes of vendors still unpacking their stuff, looking for that Stickley lamp base from grandma's house with the 90 dollar price tag, the prize that will sell within five minutes once it hits the table. *Better walk faster* was my mantra."

"Sounds like fun."

"It is for a day or so, but by the seventh day the market is five miles long. New fields opened every day. The pace is a meander by evening. Miles of kiosks, all lit up and organized, full of tables brimming with a year's accumulation of yesterday's scores. Great forests of oak chairs and deep canyons of armoires and case pieces leading into dark interiors of transport vans. Lakes of framed paintings lying face up on the grass."

"Sounds like you had your afternoons free."

"I spent afternoons in my booth. My goal was to leave with nothing but a bunch of cash in my pocket."

"Three days with no antiques on Martha's Vineyard, Lucy, with a pocketful of dusty cash and nothing to wrestle with but ideas was just the vacation I needed." Wally's eyes lost focus. Two seagulls hovered above them, looking for an unattended morsel. He didn't notice.

"Wally?" Lucy said, the wind whipping her hair.

"I never should have sold those chairs," he said.

"What are you talking about?"

"Sorry ... lost in a memory. I stumbled on a set of odd Mission chairs I'd never seen before. The price was 2,000 dollars—all the money I made the week before, the money I needed to pay the rent when I got back to the mainland. After lunch, when the class reconvened, I asked them to help me solve my dilemma. They told me to buy them because it was obvious I was going to get them anyway."

"So you bought them, then."

"Of course I bought them. Sold the lot a week later, for five grand. Worth 35,000 dollars today. Wish I kept 'em."

A loud ferry whistle signaled their arrival at the Schwartz Bay dock. Wally and Lucy joined the crowd heading toward their cars.

Below, on the vehicle deck, one of the other passengers kept the van in sight as he stepped into his rented black Ford sedan.

The Russian had no trouble keeping the blue van in sight. He watched as his quarry and the woman he had picked up on Camano Island drove into the heart of the very English city of Victoria and parked on Fort Street, a commercial row of two story business fronts.

Considering the profession of the driver, the profusion of antique stores and auction houses was not a surprise. Now wearing Northwest camouflage—a Mariners baseball cap—the Russian tilted his brim down as he sat in his parked rental and watched the pair disappear and emerge from the shops.

Each visit was brief. The dealer left the last shop, looking sad—that was new.

He followed as the pair drove across town and met a man at a sidewalk restaurant near the inlet to Victoria Harbor. That trio ate sandwiches and drank amber beer. Behind them, at the water's edge, a line of seagoing vessels floated parallel to the tourist promenade. The submarine against the dock startled him: it was a Russian K Class vessel, long outdated by the nuclear fleet, but still a sight from home. He was saddened by the sight of a proud Soviet warship reduced to a curiosity, one more chunk of the former Soviet Union for sale to the highest bidder. He longed to climb the gangplank as a common visitor to Canada and feel the presence of Mother Russia, but decided to keep the trio in sight.

The trio walked back to the van and drove north into an industrial area, parked in front of a dilapidated wood frame building on Rock Bay Road. They entered a side door. The American emerged from the building carrying a gray metal, basketball-sized globe with clear glass lenses protruding like the eyes of a Siberian potato. Many adjustable silver-colored arms held articulated mirrors. It looked like some kind of early light fixture, possibly from a surgery or a laboratory. Waving goodbye to their Canadian companion, the Americans drove away. The Russian scratched his head and started the car.

Twilight fell as the transport headed north on Canadian Route 1-A. Black electrical tape on his quarry's taillights created red-rimmed Xs that made the vehicle easy to follow as darkness swallowed the road.

Chapter Six

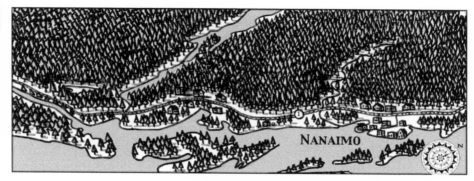

Near Nainaimo, British Columbia

"I haven't seen a motel for some time now, neighbor-man. Have you?" Lucy spoke over the throbbing of seven cylinders doing the work of eight.

"I'm looking out the same window as you, Lucy. There'll be more up ahead. Lighten up."

"Sure. Maybe that's a motel right over there, hiding behind that tree."

"This is the island's main highway north. We still have Nainaimo."

"We passed two exits for Nainaimo a few miles back."

"Darn it. That fucking bypass. That's new since the last time I was up this way. Used to be we had to drop down and drive through the center of town. How could I have missed them? I must have been daydreaming."

"It's not daytime."

"Duskdreaming, then. Campbell River is still up ahead. It's a resort fishing town. Don't worry. There'll be plenty of places to sleep.

Trust me. Anyway, the van's nearly empty and we have lots of packing blankets."

"I want my own bed."

"Don't you think it would be fun, snuggling together in back, parked by a rushing brook? I can pick up a bottle of red, carve up some beef stick. Hell, maybe a block of Canadian cheddar. It'll be like camping. I'll behave."

"And at 3 AM the snuggle goes south, Buster, I've camped with you before. Sometime during the night I'll shift my weight and you'll think it's your birthday."

Peering out into the starless, overcast night, she bent a finger against the cold windshield. "Look there!" High beams illuminated a road sign advertising the Bideawee Motor Court ahead. "I'm saved," she said.

Wally eased off the gas and resumed speed when the van rounded a curve and the neon *No Vacancy* sign came into view. "Lucy," he cooed, drawing her name into an endearment. "All full. Sorry. I guess it's you and me and the love nest on wheels." His hand reached across the gulf between them. Laughing, she slapped it away.

"There's another one, Romeo. To the right. Coming up. See it? Oh, and it has kitchenettes." Lucy said. "I love kitchenettes," she lied, looking forward to a long shower and a night in her own bed. "Looks like they have a vacancy."

Wally decelerated and hit the turn signal. "Whatever pleases you, neighbor-girl. I'm afraid I've wasted our time on this trip anyway, trying to find that swindler, Smith. No one in Victoria seems to have heard of him. If he's not known on Fort Street, we'll never locate the bastard. I've got people to look in on while we're on the island. Some old antique leads to follow up. At least we can be comfortable tonight."

In a tiny office that smelled of Pine Sol, he peeled three portraits of Queen Elizabeth off the Canadian roll he carried in his pocket. A turbaned clerk counted out the change in a handful of coins. "Loonies and Toonies, they call 'em." Wally explained the quirky Canadian slang for one- and two-dollar coins to Lucy as he tried to remember his license plate number.

"We're trying to locate a man named Smith, Don Smith," Lucy said. The owner looked at Wally and shrugged. Wally rolled his eyes at his companion as they left with the key.

"Don't look at me like that," she said. "The guy you're looking for might live way up here. We certainly didn't find him back in Victoria. It's a big island. Maybe he likes to fish." She followed Wally to the van where he gathered his new acquisition to bring inside. "Good idea," she whispered over his shoulder. "Now you've got a bed-mate tonight. Keep you out of mine."

Sitting on his bed, Wally brought the first shine in a hundred years to the light fixture's dull, nickel-silvered finish. Lucy smirked, watching her neighbor as he rubbed the lamp lovingly with one of his socks. "And you're going to wear that stocking tomorrow?" she said, amused. "You're turning it black."

"I'll turn it inside out," Wally said, admiring the shine.

Lucy shrugged. "Whatever. People sure got nervous this morning when you asked them if they knew Smith."

"That one fellow dropped a plate decorated by your people—the English. Goodbye, Queen Victoria."

"The Western world is sexually repressed today because of our virgin queen. I say *good riddance*." Lucy was almost under the covers now, a cutoff T-shirt exposing the bottoms of her breasts as she lay back.

"Doesn't seem to have affected you, naughty girl," Wally said as he shifted his gaze toward her chest.

Lucy pulled the covers to her chin and changed the subject: "And that fancy shop with the *Closed* sign on Fort Street, belonging to that fellow who died—the bloke who'd driven off the road last weekend. You say you knew him?"

"Yeah, Geoffrey. Good old Geoffrey. I've driven that old Sooke Highway. It hangs over some scary drop-offs. He should have known better."

"That one shopkeeper seemed to think it was no accident, remember?"

"Yeah, the coin dealer next to Geoffrey's store. That guy's paranoid. I've known him for years. He thinks an alien's body is still down at Roswell, New Mexico. None of the other dealers shared misgivings, if they had any. But, now that you mention it, they all acted tweaked. The guy's dead, of course they'd be upset, he was one of them, a Fort Street legend. Geoffrey was a nice guy besides. Not a lying, thieving prick like half the dealers I know. Everyone liked him. Let me tell you, that man could find good stuff. Amazing the rare objects he'd root out, especially out here on Vancouver Island. Some of us in the business used to joke that he must have gone door-knocking with a gun. Gonna miss him. Gonna miss his shop. If anyone on Fort Street knew our Mr. Smith, it would have been Geoffrey."

"No asking him now."

"Not unless you speak Ghost. Remind me to get in touch with his wife before we leave the island, will you? She could probably use a hug. There are a few things he told me he would never sell. Kept them at home, he said. Away from eyes like mine. I should let the widow know I could help if she needed a little cash to get her through the funeral."

"I've always admired you for your giving heart." Lucy said. "You want his furniture or his pottery?"

"That's cold." Wally pulled an imaginary spear from his back. "Word on the street was he had a lamp collection to die for. Funeral expenses are going through the roof, they say. Poor woman."

The Russian grazed on a boxed convenience-store salad and sipped a warm beer. He set the windup alarm for 7 AM and closed his eyes.

Chapter Seven

Campbell River, British Columbia

The sun rise the next morning was marked by a brightening in the east through a thick layer of dreary overcast as Wally and Lucy approached Campbell River.

"Cross your fingers, Lucy," he said.

Lucy held up both hands with her fingers entwined. "Why?" she asked.

"Five years ago I saw something amazing in Campbell River. A sideboard. We're going to find out if it's still in the dining room where I saw it. With a little luck, we're going to buy it and put it in my living room. I figure while we're up on the island it's worth a shot."

As the van crested a hill, Lucy looked out at miles of trees blanketing the valley before them. A range of glacier-and-purple peaks zigzagged into the low cloud layer and disappeared. The blue curve of a distant bay cut across the horizon from the right.

"I can't believe you drove all the way out here, 30 miles from the bloody Artic Circle, expecting to find something old and valuable," she said.

"It was shit luck. I'll admit it. I was really up here to go fishing. My buddy, Rudy, likes to go fishing more than anything else in the world. From upstate New York. One day, five years ago, he calls me and tells me we're going up to Campbell River, flying in on a vintage DC-3, to catch a Tyee. He's got tickets and reservations at the lodge, even a guide. My cost is 500 bucks. I say, let's go."

"Tyee ... a fish?"

"Giant salmon. Thirty-five pounds. Anyway, Rudy's a dealer, too. Hickory furniture and rustic stuff. He's a big shot in that world. Has a bunch of picture books to his credit and hangs out with movie stars. So we go out with our guide at 5 AM and catch a couple fish. Nice ones, by the way, but no Tyees. Two PM, we're back on shore with nothing to do until the next morning. Campbell River is only three streets wide, but we decided to run the town looking for antiques. It was in our blood. Silly, huh?"

"It's a disease."

"Tell me about it. Tell Rae. Tell her it's not my fault. Third street in from the water we find a furniture refinishing shop. Run by an Irishman named Jack. Johnny Cash, he tells us as soon as we go in. Johnny and him were pals way back. Back while they were both discovering the evil of drink. He shows us photos of him and the singer. All yellow and foxed. Johnny Cash and a much younger Jack. Back in his Iron Man days."

Lucy nodded.

"I asked him if there's anything interesting here in Campbell River for us to look at. Refinishers know everybody's business. He said there was a sideboard owned by a logging family. Damnedest piece he's ever seen. And he was right. It haunts me today."

Lucy didn't say anything.

"He sent us to a log house at the edge of the settlement. The old man had just lost his job at the mill, so the family might be short of cash."

The town of Campbell River looked to Wally much as the same as it had appeared five years before. The northward march of progress from Victoria, marked by strip malls and McDonald's, had petered out a hundred miles south. The fishing resort was still the most important building in Campbell River, but the grocery store in town could now sell more expensive wines.

After a two-block search, Wally found the refinishing shop, still offering stripped and lacquered highchairs and darkly varnished English tavern tables.

"Yes, the Joneses are still in town," Jack, who was a little stouter than Wally remembered, said. "It's the fourth house on the right after Cedar Street. Don't you remember? I sent you and that whiny buddy of yours over there five years back. Don't you remember?"

"I remember. I just wanted to check with you first. It's been a long time," Wally said.

"Now that the mill's closed they might be glad to see you."

"The mill was closed the last time I was here," Wally said.

"All the more reason to visit," the refinisher said.

"Have you heard of a bloke named Don Smith?" Lucy said.

Wally looked at a murky-finish tea table for sale in the showroom. Close inspection revealed a plywood top. He looked toward the door, his interest floating away like a puff of smoke.

"I know a Don Smith," the restorer said. "He's a woodworker over to Port Alberni. Strange duck. Says he makes clocks. He used to stop in once in a while when there was a hardwood sale at the mill."

Wally's head snapped up. Lucy was smiling as if she'd swallowed a canary.

"Maybe," he said, "we'll stop in to see him on the way down island."

Five years had not gone so well with the Jones family. Gone was the new pickup and camper. Small trailers that once held personal watercraft sat empty, covered with last fall's leaves. Tall, uncut grass and peeling paint suggested that the timber business was not booming. The haggard housewife who answered the door remembered the day when Wally and that fast-talking Easterner had showed up. She crossed herself and looked to the sky when Wally, fondling a handful of American cash, asked if she were interested in selling the piece of furniture today. She answered she'd have to call her husband, who was down in Victoria, looking for work. Ten minutes later the three of them loaded the heavy cabinet into the van.

The smiling woman, 1500 American dollars richer, said to Wally as he prepared to drive away, "If you're interested in the rest of the set I'll call my sister and see if she still has the table and chairs and the corner cupboard. Stop back before you leave the island."

Wally told her he had some business in Port Alberni and could come back in a couple of days.

With the tricked-out Stickley sideboard tucked away in back and a lead on the whereabouts of the mysterious consignor, Wally's mood was upbeat. Lucy, sitting cross-legged on the remaining packing blankets, was pulling one drawer out at a time, searching for a label as instructed. "Careful back there," Wally shouted over his shoulder. "Don't scratch the wood, it's the original finish."

Lucy, rocking with the motion of the tired suspension, asked, "Why exactly is this thing so great?"

47

"Stickley cabinetry is legendary, Lucy, Great finishes, hand-crafted hardware, and dead-on proportions. Another competing outfit, the Old Hickory Chair Company, made bark-covered furniture for rustic camps and cabins. Who'd have guessed that they got together a hundred years ago and collaborated on the piece you're sitting in front of?"

Lucy continued to look at the drawers.

"Rudy and I couldn't believe it. I don't believe it now, but I own it, goddamn it. I can't wait to see the other pieces."

"So you plan to come back up here after we interview Smith?"

"If you don't mind. Shouldn't take us long to find him, now that we know where he lives. I can't believe there's more of this set. Hot damn. You OK with one more detour after the interview?"

"You're the driver. I'll be delighted if you fill the van with a bunch of bark-covered furniture. There'll be no more discussion about sleeping in back. Besides," she said coyly, "as your girlfriend said, I don't have a life."

The black rented Ford sedan blended into the sparse upcountry traffic as it followed them out of town.

Chapter Eight

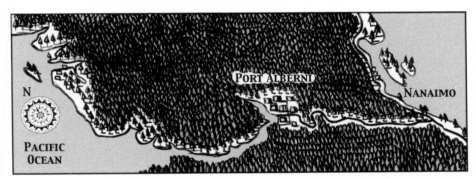

Port Alberni, British Columbia

Compared to the strip mall sprawl that crept north from Victoria, the town Wally and Lucy drove into late that afternoon felt old and genuine. Three story false-front buildings on Argile Street, once the pride of Vancouver Island, now held a cluster of antique stores, used-clothing malls and taverns, the inheritors of a dying historic region. Low rent gypsies, knickknack shops, and dollar stores ruled the city core. Wally parked beside the Bread of Life soup kitchen and locked the doors to the van.

"Let's split up and run both sides of the street," he said. "If we find Smith and get an interview, we can wrap this up by tonight."

"I'll find him, my dear, you take this side and I'll investigate the used clothing stores across the street, looking for clues. First one to find Mr. Smith wins." Lucy danced across the empty boulevard like a schoolgirl.

Wally went to work.

As he walked past the King Edward Hotel, he looked up into glass-less window frames and squinted into the dark interior, searching for remnants of old brass fixtures. He saw gutted, empty holes waiting for prosperity to return. With his expectation antenna turned down, he entered the consignment shop on the opposite corner. It was a frightening collection of useless castaways from hardscrabble lives. Wally wandered through wooden shelves of what he considered waste-of-time china—gift-shop saucers displaying brown transfer portraits of the Queen, or *Greetings from Qualicom Beach*. Glass containers that once held wax candles, empty now, pretending to be collectible, all marked at 50 cents. Amused, he picked up a toilet paper holder from Tennessee, which held a ratty corncob and advertised, In case of emergency, break glass.

Wally bought that one. It reminded him of the love affair he had with bathroom collectibles when he was buying and selling back East.

Brasscrafters was the imprint to look for when searching for toilet paper holders in New England. Brasscrafter-signed nickel-plated paper holders and soap dishes were the Tiffany Studios of bathroom collectibles. Highlight of Wally's odd collection in those days was a wall-mounted mahogany music box that played "Whistle While You Work" as the paper left the roll.

"Do you know where I can find a fellow named Don Smith?" Wally asked as he peeled off a US 20 to pay for the corncob souvenir and a logging tintype in a gutta-percha case.

"No, no, I don't believe I know the man," the shopkeeper said. He seemed eager to conclude the sale, even waiving the tax for the cash. With nervous urgency, he ushered Wally to the front door and closed it behind him and shut off the lights.

Wally got no further in the other three junk stores on Argile Street, nothing interesting turning up except a 20s folk-art wall sign advertising paint brushes. It had original examples of the different brush styles hanging from five metal hooks. Wally had a love affair with creative, turn-of-the-century advertising. High-end dealers, regardless of their specialty, collect old trade signs like trophies. When he visited the homes of antique traders he respected, these coveted items were never for sale. He planned to keep the paint brush display for the same reason, another "fuck you" to rival dealers allowed into his home. The crabby proprietor was about to name a price when Wally mentioned Smith. The man's demeanor changed abruptly.

"Why are you asking?" He was guarded, nervous. Maybe angry.

"I'm writing a magazine article—"

"Get out."

"Wait a minute," Wally said, watching his brush-maker sign float away. "I'd like to buy your sign. How much do you want? I have cash, American cash."

He was reaching into his pocket to pull out the California roll, Hamilton-faced hundreds on top, when the shopkeeper pushed Wally. Hands in pockets, he fell.

"Hey!" Wally shouted as he lost his balance and tumbled to the floor. Leaping up, he looked into the face of a man in fear. He backed toward the door.

"Get out. I have nothing to say."

"I was willing to pay whatever you wanted for that brush sign," Wally countered weakly as he fled to the safety of Argile Street.

Lucy wasn't doing any better. Though she'd picked up two wonderfully colorful miniskirts with Carnaby Street labels and a chunky bracelet with hand-carved Bakelite fruit, she hadn't found anyone in Port Alberni who had heard of Smith.

"We ought to look for a place to stay here tonight, neighbor-man," she suggested. She was wearing one of the 60s creations she'd just found.

"Good thought," Wally said, scanning the street for motel signs, seeing none this close to the city center. He didn't consider sleeping at the King Edward Hotel, which seemed to be open despite the lack of glass in the windows. They passed on a chance to stay in the Arlington Hotel two blocks closer to the shoreline. It advertised itself as the *Fun Spot on Northport*, and sported the Paul Bunyan Lounge.

"This is a big sport fishing area," he said to Lucy, steering her toward the van. "I'm sure we'll find something with clean sheets down by the water. Hey, that's a nice dress."

Two hours later, they left their room at the Jolly Fisherman Motor Court on Front Street, next to the slumbering Weyerhaeuser mill. They walked through late-afternoon shadows of silent smokestacks, searching for a tavern and some food.

The Russian took a room at the opposite end of the motor court. He opened the drapes, moved an armchair near the window, and sat down. The rearview mirror borrowed from the rental car and taped to the porch support outside reflected the parking lot. He stood up and walked out into the silence of a lazy spring afternoon to adjust the angle.

Chapter Nine

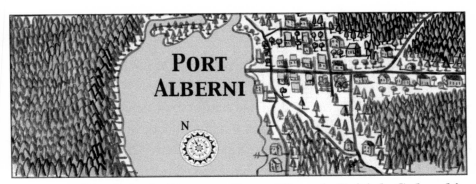

Big John's Tavern, Port Alberni, British Columbia

Wally and Lucy occupied a booth near the back of a watering hole called Big John's, under the street level on the side of the Beaufort Hotel. Nice part of town, Wally thought. Across from the Salvation Army Store.

After a burger, a beer, and two pool games, Wally wanted to ask the men in the booth behind them about Smith, but Lucy was holding the floor.

"So here I was," Lucy confided to a pair of Canadian boys behind her in the next booth. "Sitting in a second floor flat in London with five other ladies, all talking dirty and moaning. We're all on our telephones, drinking tea and smoking cigarettes, having a little game about who could get our customer off first. My guy was into feet, so I'm pretending to sniff one of my shoes which I claim has a long spiked heel, when I'm actually wearing tennies."

The room reeked of stale tobacco rising from a rat-hair orange shag carpet matted with dark shiny spots from ancient accidents. It sported posters of hockey players attached to the smoke-blackened knotty pine wall with Scotch tape.

Kirk McLean, Theo Fleury, and Brian Heyward, they were told, were local heroes. Helmeted and padded, the icons struck their aggressive poses on their skates, former supermen to a generation of Canadian boys.

Lucy, wearing her new flower-power miniskirt, had lost both games of eight ball to Wally.

The two tavern regulars had hardly expected an inside glimpse at the world of London phone sex when they stopped in at Big John's that evening. Lucy had their booth-neighbors, a pair of beer-drinking young men who looked to Wally like loggers or truck drivers, listening to every word.

"Myrna was the best," she said. "She was quite beautiful, ironically, for a phone sex mate. Five-foot two, platinum blond hair down to her ass. All the masochists asked for her. They loved getting scolded in her little-girl voice. We got paid by the call, you know. The clients gave us their Visa number and expiration date. We'd verify it and call them back. The Visa company hated us. They knew we were dodgy, even though we claimed the numbers were for mail order." She smiled.

"By the way," she added, having reached deeper into the Port Alberni psyche than a team of private investigators could have, "have any of you heard of a fellow named Don Smith?"

"I know the son of a bitch," said the older one, who sported a handlebar mustache and an Australian drawl. "I delivered hardwood slabs to him at the clock shop out on the bay."

"They make fakes out there," said his more stout and gnarly-featured friend. He looked startled when Wally Winchester's head snapped up so quickly. "Yeah, they make those grandfather clocks that look like the old ones."

54

"Those are called reproductions, moron," corrected the Australian.

"Well, they look like fakes to me," said the second fellow who, Wally figured, had never been farther south than Victoria and did not want to lose points in Lucy's eyes.

"Actually," said his more worldly partner, "it's pretty amazing, the things I've delivered there. Ever heard of Honduras mahogany, ebony?"

"Damn foreign wood," snorted the logger. "No wonder we're out of work."

"The point is that all the clocks you see there in Smith's shop are made of Doug fir."

Lucy's eyes opened slightly at the revelations, encouraging his every word. The Australian plowed ahead with his conversation: "I delivered other stuff. Gold and silver and a pretty fancy bunch of woodworking gear."

"Well, I still say they're fakes." The local was rapidly losing the battle for Lucy's heart, and he probably knew it. "I've seen some foreign fellers there. I don't like foreigners."

He looked at his rival. The beer and testosterone were kicking in. Wally sensed it was time to get his partner home.

"How do you get to this clock shop?" he asked.

At the opposite end of the bar, near the front door, a man with a three-day beard and new hat advertising the Frontier Days Logging Rodeo had melted into the tavern woodwork. He nursed a vodka shot, neat, as he watched the Englishwoman's antics from a distance, unable to hear her conversation. She was animated as she talked, eyes flashing, hands dancing, head bobbing, controlling the moment. He studied her face, the way her brown locks framed a pointed English chin and a Roman nose.

He rubbed his tired eyes. The woman's role in this affair was still unclear, but it was obvious that, at least here in the Canadian bar, she was in charge.

Chapter Ten

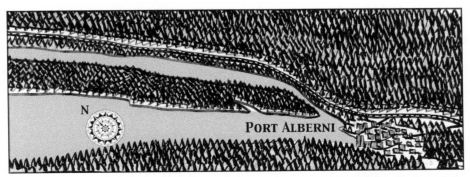

West of Port Alberni, British Columbia

The road to Don Smith's clock shop wound west toward Tofino over hills and gullies on the shore of Barkley Sound. The sun had finally emerged from the early morning fog. They passed two antique shops on the right. Wally smiled as he looked back in the side mirror.

"A guy in that antique shop there, Lucy, once turned me onto a set of chairs worth 200,000 dollars. If he's open on the way back I'd like to stop and thank him."

"Wally, we're a hundred miles up in the middle of an island in a foreign country. Do you have a relationship with everybody up here?"

"I'd never bought anything in this guy's shop. He offered dumb English mahogany reproductions, but when I'm antique picking this far from home I stop at every shop I run across. 'Cause you never know. One time up here he says to me, I saw a couple of the kind of chairs you're looking for. I asked him if they were Stickley."

Wally glanced at Lucy, then back to the road.

"He told me no and opened a book of 20th century design and showed me a photo of a Charles Rennie Mackintosh teahouse chair from about 1903, a hundred-year-old design so modern it was used in a *Star Trek* episode. That's modern. Ever heard of him? He started the Glasgow School."

Lucy looked back at the storefront, disappearing behind a bend in the road.

"Everybody in the British Isles knows Mackintosh design. I've been to the Victoria and Albert Museum. I've seen his furniture. I can't believe one of his chairs ended up way out here on the Pacific Coast of Canada."

"Neither could I, believe me. He told me an Englishman bought a hotel in Winnipeg and filled the lobby with antiques from his own collection. Said a pair of these chairs sat in a mezzanine waiting area. One of the chairs was wobbly, needed to be re-glued. That wobbly part jazzed me up 'cause they were reproducing that model by then as classic furniture. Wobbly meant it might really be an original. It also explained why these treasures could have found their way into western Canada."

Lucy said, "Two hundred thousand? Did you get them? They're not in your house. I would have noticed."

"I don't have the chairs. Not yet," Wally said, driving slowly as they looked for signs of a clock shop. "Let me get back to the story. The next week I called the hotel and had a woman at the front desk look up in the mezzanine for the chairs. She told me there weren't any chairs there, none that she'd ever seen. I asked how long she'd worked there. Seven years. I asked if any employees still around had worked there back in 1990 when the fellow remembered seeing them. The clerk said none that she knew about."

"Sounds like a dead end," Lucy said.

"There are no dead ends, Kiddo, just detours. I asked the desk clerk to check around and I'd call her back. She called me half an hour later and referred me to a former assistant manager working in the main office in Toronto. I called that gal, careful not to reveal to an executive in the hotel chain that I planned to sweet-talk her organization out of a prize that they didn't know they had. Made up a story that I'd been there on my honeymoon in 1990 and wanted to know if the old hotel looked the same."

"She bought that story?"

"Actually she didn't. Started questioning me about my interest. I told her my wife had cancer. She wanted us to be photographed in the chairs where we sipped champagne after our wedding. Sort of a last memory."

"That's cold."

"Worked. She told me that she remembered the chairs. Said they'd been taken into a storeroom after one fell apart. Now I knew they were old. I told her it was breast cancer. She said she'd make a call—"

"There's the sign," Lucy shouted. A white-painted rectangle, nailed to a tree across the road, announced *Phoenix Industries*. It marked a gravel drive down to the water's edge. Wally wheeled the van left across the empty eastbound lane and entered the shadow of a second-growth forest.

Chapter Eleven

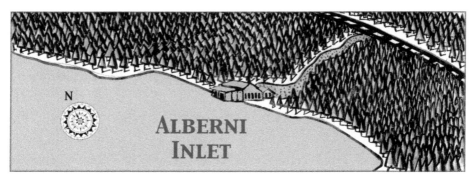

Phoenix Industries Woodshop, Port Alberni,
British Columbia

A big old building, its back to Barkley Sound, appeared after a bend in the drive. Wally counted six vehicles in the parking lot: a beefed-up SUV, three Mercedes sedans and a pair of weather-beaten pickup trucks. The German sedans were probably out of place at a modest clock shop halfway to the North Pole, but his radar was on low. The thought dissolved in a mind weary from three days on the road. He had decided his interview idea was turning into a pain-in-the-ass goose chase and he looked forward to heading for home.

Parking the van under a mossy cedar giant at the edge of the parking lot, Wally and Lucy walked toward the building's unmarked office door. Wally turned the doorknob, found it unlocked, and walked in.

He felt old spirits in the room. The walls were wide, rough-cut old-growth boards. A waist-high counter stood in front of an inner door. Eight wooden clocks hung from hooks on the wall behind it. A Black Forest-type grandfather's tall clock stood against the wall in the waiting room, which offered seating on two mismatched local chairs.

Lucy rang the brass desk bell. No one appeared. Wally inspected the clocks. They were not the works of master craftsmen. At best, they were hobby projects on a good day. The joinery was not clean and there was little or no ornamentation, save some simple band-saw cutouts on the crest. They looked like the work of a senior center woodshop class.

The rear door finally opened and a high cheek-boned tough wearing a shop apron appeared. Sawdust speckled his short blond hair and shirt. "What do you want?"

Wally put on his most upbeat persona. He said, "I'm looking for Don Smith. I'm told I can find him here."

"What is your business?" The accent sounded German.

"We have a clock that you people made and it keeps terrible time," Lucy said, jumping up to the counter beside Wally. "We want to return it or have it repaired."

Wally smiled and lifted his thumb at his side in a subtle salute.

The German said, "I will get him. Wait here," as he marched out of the room.

The gray-haired, bearded 60-ish fellow, wearing a tweed jacket, was the man Wally remembered from the auction. He seemed frailer than the week before. Entering from the door behind the counter, he looked as if he hadn't slept.

"What can I do for you?" There was wariness in his voice.

"Hi, my name is Walter Winchester, and this is my associate Lucy Adams. I'm writing a magazine article about the John Townsend writing desk. It would really help me if I can ask you a few questions."

Smith's eyes never left Wally's as he made his request, but Smith's hands trembled noticeably. His voice quavered. "I remember you from the auction. You bought my table. I have nothing to say to you. Please leave."

Wally tried to read the man's eyes and got nowhere. He wondered how hard to push and decided to let it rip. The worst thing that could happen was that they would go home with no story.

"It really means a lot to me, Don. This is my big chance to write a feature story. I'd do anything, pay anything, for a chance to write this correctly. Besides, don't you want to present your side of the story in my article?"

"Let me say this clearly," Smith looked into Wally's eyes. "Get the bloody hell out of this building. If you persist in this foolish pursuit you will be putting your life in peril."

There was no graceful exit. Just retreat. As they backed out the door into the parking lot, Wally noticed a major power line, visible only in the clearing next to the outside wall, emerge from the fir trees and entered the building. The thick cable fed into a tall metal cabinet, stenciled *Danger: High Voltage* in regulation yellow.

Lot of power for a clock shop, Wally thought, shaking his hands as if they were wet to rid himself of the palpable creepiness in the clock shop. He wondered about the two surveillance cameras in the office and the high-tech security console on the wall.

Standing flat against the faded clapboard exterior, the Russian watched the meeting through the dirty office window. He had been visibly startled when he watched the consignor from the auction open an interior door and step up to the counter. He saw an angry exchange and retreated to the shrubbery as the pair left.

As the man and woman climbed into the van, the Russian dashed up the steep forested hill to his rental car. He was finishing the remnants of a bad, upcountry submarine sandwich washed down with cold coffee as the subject van lurched out into the road and headed back toward Port Alberni.

Spitting gravel behind it, the van turned east. Wally was wired. He said, "Look for a turnout. Find me a place to pull the van over."

The Russian watched his side view mirror and saw the blue Dodge van round the curve. The vehicle passed his parked rental and headed back toward Port Alberni.

"Okay, my friend," he whispered. "We will see where your conspiracy will lead."

A roadside rest area appeared at the next turn. Wally pulled in, shut the lights off, and parked.

Lucy spoke first. "What happened in there? I vote to forget the story. The man's a nut case. No magazine article is worth this much weirdness."

"I've got to go back and see if there's a window or two that I can look in," Wally said, wondering whose voice was coming through his mouth. "Something else is going on in that building."

"I think he made it pretty clear in the office, don't you?" Lucy said.

"Wait here. Give me one hour. If I'm not back by then, drive to Port Alberni and call the police. I'd rather take my chances with the Mounties."

"I vote for going antiquing and giving this silly project up," she said. "But I'll back you up with the hour wait if that's what you really want to do."

"I'll be fine. See you in 30 minutes."

Pulling a dark windbreaker over his light shirt as he jogged, Wally headed back up the road west to find a woodland route to the former cannery.

The Russian had no time to ponder the conspiracy angles as the van veered into a parking area only half a kilometer east of the clock shop. The right turn caught him, as the Americans called it, *flatfooted.* Driving past the quarry vehicle as it parked, he found a wide shoulder farther down the road and pulled over, double-timing it back to the parking spot in time to observe the Camano Island man walking cautiously back toward the clock factory. He was easy to follow.

Twenty-five feet past the dirt road to the shop, Wally stepped into the woods and headed for Barkley Sound. Fearing surveillance that covered the gravel road, he kept to the underbrush. Blackberry brambles pulled at his clothes. The forest opened up to his right. Gratefully, he moved into the clearing, a cathedral of tall Douglas firs, strolling easily through the manicured floor that only a mature Northwest forest can create. Soggy, spongy timber from old windfalls was a soundless rolling carpet underfoot, all the way to the water and the mysterious building. He spotted a camera on the roof over the entry door he'd just left and kept to the woods, angling toward the side windows.

Ninety years of paint and ocean salt formed a faded yellow crackle coating on the old-growth boards. Alert for another camera, Wally headed for the west corner, thinking the chances for a peek inside would be better down by the water. A wall full of windows continued 25 feet out over the sound onto a dock, but the land dropped steeply toward the water. Poking around on the shore for something to stand on, excruciating pain in his left ear nearly brought him to his knees.

"*YEEEEEEEEEOWWWWW!*" erupted from Wally.

"I did not think we would see you again, my friend." The tough-faced German grasped Wally's earlobe in a fierce upward twist.

It hurt.

The German's face showed no emotion as he used that terrible earlobe kink to lead Wally up the hill on the gravel drive. "Where is your vehicle, asshole?"

"It's down around the corner at a rest area," Wally said.

The pain in his head was unending as the German twisted harder.

"Do I have to walk down the road with you like this or would you listen to a very clear statement?"

"I'll take the very clear statement."

"Get out, or you are dead."

The German let go of Wally's ear and launched a wicked kick that caught him squarely in the buttock. The secession of ear-pain blended smartly with an unpleasant throbbing in his rear. Wally was 30 yards down the road before he had his first clear thought.

I give up, he proclaimed inside his head. Time to go back to normal life. Sorry, *Art and Antiques Magazine*, I guess it's not my time. He was still rubbing the pain out of his left ear as he opened the van door. Lucy was nodding to 30s blues music on the BBC. He was 35 minutes early. They drove away without saying a single word.

Nothing the Russian had just witnessed made any sense. If I were watching a conspiracy unfold, he told himself, why did the dealer sneak back to the old boathouse to snoop around? More confusing still was the ear-pulling scene that left the man standing back on the road, rubbing the side of his head. A falling-out between thieves? He doubted it. The ear-puller was a stranger to the dealer. The body language was clear. As the old van pulled out of the parking area, he hurried to his car.

Chapter Twelve

East of Port Alberni, British Columbia

The road east dropped sharply and rose again just as steeply as it wound through a mountainous clear-cut area deep in the middle of Vancouver Island. Weird ugliness settled into the pit of Wally's stomach. Their adventure had gone too far. They passed the open antique shop where the owner had turned Wally on to a pair of Mackintosh chairs. It was open. Wally didn't flinch as he drove by.

"Not stopping to see your friend?"

"I just want to go home."

"Well," Lucy said, "finish your story. Did you go and find those chairs?"

"My ear is killing me," Wally said. "My butt hurts and I'm mad as hell. Don't know if I feel like talking right now. Did you bring a gun?"

"Of course, darling," she said, stretching the endearment into a Hollywood cliché. "I smuggled it across the border. Tell me the end of your hotel chair story. You always brighten up when you get to talk about yourself."

"So me and Rae are just getting to know each other," Wally began. "I figured we'd go check out the hotel in Winnipeg. Try to find the chairs, show her a little about the life, you know, a three-day trip through beautiful country, antiquing all day, nice dinners in new towns, exotic motels, just like tourists."

Wally was following a truck filled with five-foot-diameter logs. The heavy vehicle was racing down the steep two-lane inclines, then slowing to 10 miles an hour as it pulled its load up the other side toward the next ridge top. Another truck closed the distance behind Wally's van, looming in his the rearview mirror. Wally was unnerved by the aggressive driving, but he had a story to finish.

"So we get to this hotel and it's 14 stories. I was expecting a turn-of-the-century landmark with a pair of break-your-heart chairs hidden inside, not a skyscraper, but we'd driven two days to get there so we checked in anyway. The room charge was 250 bucks a night. Next morning, I find out that it's Canada Day and the hotel's running on a skeleton crew. No manager. He's on vacation. No assistant manager. Same story. You want permission to go into our storerooms? No. Then a busted pipe flooded the dining room with gray water an hour after we got to our room. No weekend dining. Everybody I asked to let me into the storeroom looked at me like I was out of my fucking mind." Wally accelerated past the truck in front as it pulled over to the shoulder and parked. "I'll get back to Winnipeg someday."

Bump. Wally was trying not to brake too much on the alarming downward switchback when he felt the impact. Lucy's startled expression said she felt it, too.

BUMP. It was deliberate, for sure, stronger this time. The semi's grill was a hulking monster at their backs.

"Buckle up, goddammit!" Wally shouted over the squeal of his brakes, the big diesel throbbing on his bumper, and a guitar riff on the radio.

BUMP. Wally put his foot on the brake pedal and felt 10,000 pounds of Detroit diesel roaring in pursuit. Wally could barely control his van. The road dropped in a long, steep left _-turn and up the other side of the mountain ridge. Good sense said slow down and take this hairpin in low, but the irresistible force at the rear bumper said, I'm gonna drive you off the road.

Wally shouted, "This guy is gonna kill us!" Lucy was pale, buckled in tightly.

The valley floor moved in slow motion a thousand feet below.

If I can get past that hairpin turn, Wally thought wildly, I can lose him on the incline. He quickly scanned the road cutting diagonally up the mountain's opposite slope. It looked clear, no traffic coming from the other direction.

That's good. Panic filled his chest. The hairpin came up too fast. He stood on the shuddering brake pedal, but the van still did not slow. He bit his lip, jammed his foot hard on the accelerator. A gap opened behind him and his attacker. The hairpin curve loomed closer.

Lucy sank into her center where the world and her spirit met. It didn't completely shut out her exponentially increasing fear as Wally sped into a near-90 degree turn. "What the fuck?" she screamed.

"Shut up a minute. I know what I'm doing," Wally lied. Wally tapped the brakes and the van fishtailed wildly. He cut to the left onto the oncoming lane as they hit the hairpin. The landscape tipped as the left wheels rose off the pavement. Wally and Lucy leaned toward the driver's door in an instinctive but useless sailboat gesture to inertia. The rustic sideboard and the nickel-plated fixture bounced around freely in the back of the van. "You fucker!" Wally yelled, surprised at how much mental energy he was devoting to the damage to the furniture behind him. The left wheels slammed back onto hardtop and the van swerved and skidded again, sending pebbles over the precipice on the left. The incline up the other side was steep and the van slowed, so Wally glanced in the side mirror. Behind him, a truck full of logs trailed a dense white plume of vaporizing brake pads. The weight of the truck and the load were finally working against their attacker.

Lucy, rousing from her torpor, shouted. "There's a viewpoint up ahead on the top of the hill, remember? We talked about it first time round. You made a joke."

"Yeah, the piss spot with a view. We laughed about it."

"You laughed about it, Wally."

"It was my joke."

Exhilaration boosted them up the hill at top speed, leaving the attacker farther and farther behind. The road crested the hill, curved sharply right as it followed the mountain shoulder. Ahead, at the top, Wally saw a road-cut to the side. Brakes and tires squealing, he steered the van across the oncoming lane at 45 miles an hour, cutting off a startled driver cresting the hill from the opposite direction. He careened wildly behind them and fought for control. Wally skidded into the parking lot. The van careened into a 50-foot open space that promised a terrifying drop at the far end. Two pickups with campers were in the shuddering van's path. Wally pulled hard on the wheel to miss the closest one, nearly flipping his van again. Ten feet from the line of boulders that marked an 80-degree plunge to the valley floor, the van shuddered to a stop.

A cloud of dust caught up with the van and briefly covered it from view. Engines roared as the campers fled, leaving Wally's vehicle sitting alone. He turned off the ignition, killing the engine and the radio. He listened. Silence. The faint whine of an invisible airliner broke the spell.

"Well, that was fun," Lucy said after half a minute of quiet breathing. They sat, hidden from the road, concealed by the road-cut wall. "Nice going," Lucy said, wide eyes contrasting with her calm voice. A loud, chugging diesel rose and fell as an 18-wheeler crested the shoulder behind the cliff-side turn. The noise diminished as the vehicle continued east behind the hill.

"Might have been our guy. Probably was," Wally said. "That son-of-a-bitch."

Anger and relief bounced around, unspoken, in the van.

"Do you think he did that on purpose?" Lucy asked.

"Maybe he lost his brakes. It still makes him an asshole. He scared the living shit out of me! Let's go back to Camano Island, where the most dangerous places have hot water in them."

"Sign me up, mate."

The nose of the Dodge van ventured out slowly where the viewpoint entrance road opened onto the highway. Driving against the directional arrows in the entrance road, Wally hesitated at the entrance. He looked right and left and right again. Their attacker was nowhere in sight.

There was no doubt that the truck driver had tried to kill the people in the van. The Russian had watched the episode unfold from his quarter-mile drop back on the lightly traveled Route Four. The 18-wheeled vehicle had cut him off in its haste to get behind the van. After the Dodge righted itself at the bottom of the hairpin curve, the Russian lost sight of it. Blinded by brake fog and stuck behind the malevolent logger and his 20,000 pounds of old-growth cedar, he cursed fluently in Russian. The blue van was nowhere to be seen when he got over the ridge to the other side.

Military logic took over. Based on what he'd observed, he figured he'd spot the American's van in the parking lot of some antique shop on the road ahead. He expected they would head south once on the Victoria highway, so he knew the route he'd travel. Every roadside village he encountered on Route Four, especially those advertising antique shops, would be searched. They had a five-minute head start on an almost one-way road. The Russian was confident he'd see them soon on this mountain highway.

He found the blue van in the second town to the east, a quiet village called Oak Hill: three antique shops at a crossroad with a gas station, a fossil store, a burger stand advertising vinegar fries, and a tourist stop called Wing World. The parking lot for Wing World was long and deep, filled with motor homes and pickup truck campers with trailers. He almost missed Wally's blue van, parked nose-in, between an Airstream trailer rig and a 30-foot Winnebago. A plaque on the back announced: *We're Spending Our Grandchildren's Inheritance.*

He sighed, relieved, as he turned in and parked with a view of the vehicle. He debated keeping the van in sight versus following up inside and chose the latter. There had to be a pattern in their decisions that lent a clue to the conspiracy he pursued.

He entered the gift shop lobby and pretended to study a shelf of stuffed iguanas, euthanized by caring natives in Guatemala, for sale at six dollars apiece, as he looked for the American. The aisles were empty. He paid his eight Canadian dollar entry fee and walked into the warm, humid tropical gardens.

In a spacious, open, gossamer-roofed flower garden full of North American butterflies free to come and go as they pleased, he walked casually through glass cases where other, rarer insects fluttered aimlessly. He studied the people. He saw overweight tourists wearing matching silk jackets with names like Ned or Peggy embroidered on the sleeves. The antique dealer, Winchester, looked much more like the moths than the butterflies. During four days of observation, the Russian had noted the man's preference for tacky T-shirts. The ragged hole through his back jeans pocket identified them as the same ones he wore in the States. Whether he had brought along a change of socks and underwear was anybody's guess.

The British woman was another story. She was intriguing. She was the butterfly. He was sure she understood the concept completely. He smiled, thinking of the pool game he'd watched the evening before in Port Alberni, where he watched her gather males around her like moths to her flame.

The British woman was standing alone in the spacious open-air insectarium wearing a bright yellow miniskirt. He noticed other males watch her movements, some openly, some less so. A muscular thirtyish man, wearing a plain white car coat, his stance alert, one the Russian had used himself from time to time. A UN investigator, trained by the Russian intelligence service, could not mistake White Coat's surveillance behavior. The Russian tugged down on his cap and moved closer to the odd double agenda in the room.

White Coat held his left arm under his jacket by the belt line. This was to be an assassination, here among the silk-jacketed tourists of Wing World. The arm came up, holding a Glock with a silencer. There wasn't time to reach White Coat from behind the large glass display case between them. The Russian pressed hard against the upper part of the case and felt it move. With a leap and a heave, he tipped the vitrine off its pedestal, its metal frame striking the assassin on the shoulder as he prepared to fire. The case buckled and broke, exploding in shattering glass and fleeing butterflies. The muffled gunshot report was lost in the crash. Pupas and mock vegetation clattered against the concrete floor. The errant round struck and collapsed another glass display case right beside the British woman. One of the tall posts supporting the plastic-wrap roof collapsed and opened the tropical paradise to the clear Canadian afternoon. Rare, lovely butterflies were freed from human confinement into the real world beyond. Screaming tourists scattered and ran for the safety of their traveling four-wheel nests. Attendants with butterfly nets made frantic gestures to capture the Malaysian Diamondback Night Moth and other soon-to-be-bird food Lepidoptera that had been the pride of Western Canadian entomologists.

White Coat was gone, hidden amid the moving sea of butterfly lovers. The unwitting American antique dealer and the British woman were still in view, apparently safe, laughing impolitely to themselves under a tattered canopy of escaping dreams.

Lucy was still smiling at the events of her day. True, she thought, there were tiny cuts on her ankles where glass shards had sliced her flesh, but what a treat it had been watching absolutely stunning butterflies fleeing confinement and escaping into an endless blue sky. She looked up to see dark bands of approaching birds and silently wished the insects safe passage.

She still didn't know what caused the first glass case to fall, since her back had been turned, but the butterfly container to her right had simply disintegrated before her eyes, showering her feet with flying glass. She chalked it up to the angry hand of the butterfly gods.

Three miles east of Coombs, the cross-island highway finally met the north-south highway at a T-junction near the Nanaimo shoreline. Wally turned right toward Victoria and the ferry.

Lucy said, pointing past his ear, "What about that woman, the sister with more of that tree-trunk furniture? Campbell River's that away, isn't it?"

"Those things never pan out," he said. "I get promises like that all the time. I want off this island."

Chapter Thirteen

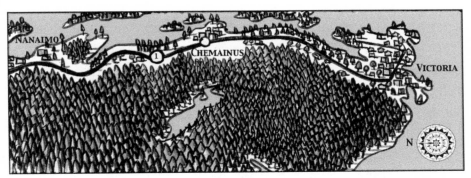

Chemainus, British Columbia

Three hours of silence ended near the exit for the village of Chemainus, 72 kilometers north of Victoria. As Wally indicated a turn he said, "This is a cool old town, Lucy, all kinds of murals. Need a break?"

She nodded.

"Twenty years ago a bunch of artists moved here and started painting the entire town. You'll see, it's a trip." Parking a few blocks from a cluster of vintage buildings, Wally pointed at the side of a bakery across the street. Lucy gazed at 40 feet of logging history painted over the cinderblock façade. The artist was accomplished, capturing with bright colors the story of Chinese workers. As they strolled, she saw other tableaus celebrating clear-cutting and mining. Joe's Pro Hardware was the canvas for European views of the lives of the First People. Bonnie Martin's Homemade Meat Pies sported a building-sized mural of the early lives of the Canadian fishermen. The façade of a tired antique store told the story of the canneries, processing the abundant salmon runs of the last century.

North of a vast painting of a timber-framed trestle carrying log trains, Wally led Lucy past his waiting Dodge van toward a tree-lined lane of old Craftsman Bungalows.

She saw where he was headed: a bright red cottage with a wrap-around porch. A yellow plywood square planted in the lawn said, *Antiques*. Wally cursed at the *Closed* sign on the door. "Too bad," he said. "The gal runs this place always has a nice collection of Parrish prints. Usually tells me she sold a Stickley piece the month before, though I've never found furniture in her shop. I think she has a thing for me, tells me tales of stuff she's heard about, hoping I'll stop again on the next trip."

Walking down the front walk toward the van, he was unprepared for a sudden jolt of pain. The voice in his ear was deep, accented, but clear and malicious.

"Get into this vehicle now or I will kill you here. I have a gun."

"What vehicle?" A smack across the back of Wally's cranium was the answer. He saw a white four-wheel-drive Jeep, door open, waiting at the curb. Another blow to his head and a jab from something solid against his shoulder blade urged him to move.

"And the girl also. Move!" A hand and arm reached down beside Wally and opened the passenger door. "Get in," he yelled to Lucy, "and you—you drive … now! Do not turn around!"

Wally's mind was searching for a way out. Would he shoot me here? In a tourist town filled with people? Well, he hasn't had a big problem kidnapping me here ... Fuck, fuck, fuck! Think of something, Wally, come on—

"Get in, piece of shit." Wally saw no help on the quiet street. He could only obey.

The sound was solid, a muffled ping … a softball sound Wally recognized. He turned to see his assailant collapse. Their rescuer was a thin man, about six feet tall, gaunt but handsome, with a softball bat in

76

his hand. He wore a blue Seattle Mariners baseball cap, tilted down. The face was familiar.

"Get in your vehicle and follow me," he said in English, his Russian accent thick. "Please. I can help you. Follow me to where we can talk. There is much I need to know if I am to help you escape from some very angry people."

Lucy tugged on Wally's sleeve, steering him toward the van. "Come on, Wally," she said. "Get it together. The bloke just saved our lives." Glancing back at the unconscious form on the sidewalk, Wally climbed unsteadily into the driver's seat. He followed as the black Ford sedan pulled out in front.

Two miles toward Victoria, the man parked the Ford at a roadside café and left room for the van behind it. He escorted them in, looked around carefully, and chose a table away from the window. He ordered three coffees and locked Wally's attention with his eyes.

"What is your connection with Don Smith and this auction in Tacoma?" He spoke quietly, carefully choosing his English words.

"Aha! That's where I know you from." Wally exclaimed, nearly spilling his mug. "The auction last week in Tacoma. You're the Russian! You liked the tangerine juice."

"Best I have tasted in the world." His crooked mouth moved in the direction of a smile.

"The Mariners hat, the shirt. You look like a Canuck. I never expected to see *you* again. Holy shit, Sherlock, what are you doing way up here?"

"Saving your life, Mr. Winchester," the Russian said, filing the phrase, *Holy shit, Sherlock*, away for his slang collection.

"Who are you and what are you doing here?" Lucy asked.

"I work for UNESCO as an investigator of stolen art." He handed his passport and UN Employee ID across the table. He held out his hand, first to the woman, looking embarrassed. "How rude of me not to introduce myself to you when we first met. I was brought up to be more of a gentleman. My name is Yvgeney Ivanchenko."

"Lucy Adams," she smiled. "The first time we met was a few moments ago, when you were wiping blonde hair off your baseball bat. I can live with that." His rough, calloused grip pleased her.

"Walter Winchester." Wally shoe-horned his introduction in.

Yvgeney, his attention on the woman, shook Wally's hand. "I know," he said to Wally as he looked at Lucy, "I have read your file. Lucy, a family name?"

"I was born just after my mother saw *I Love Lucy* on the telly."

"Interesting choice," the homesick Muscovite said, looking into her deep, dark eyes. "I have many questions but I am starving. First we have to eat." Yvgeney waved the waitress over. "I have been catching scraps of sandwiches and dinners out of a grocery sack for five days now. At least once I would like to get to the bottom of a plate."

"So you really never met Smith before the auction?" Yvgeney asked. A demolished plate of *nachos grande* sat nearby. An order of dry Canadian cheeseburger served with vinegar fries and oddly spiced brown gravy had come and gone.

"No, everyone there was a stranger, except for the auctioneer and his wife. Oddest auction I ever attended, and I beat Brown out of a sweet Chippendale table." Wally told Yvgeney the press pass story.

"And you really came all the way up here to interview this Smith for a magazine that you do not even work for?" Yvgeney said, one eye on the woman across the table as he waited for the man's response.

"Why not?" Wally said. "Wait till you see what I've got in the van. I'm always looking for excuse to go picking in Canada. The dollar goes so much further here. Why do you care about any of this?" He wiped his mouth with his sleeve. "By the way, there's something fishy going on in that clock shop. Something a lot bigger than clocks."

"I know," the Russian said. "I think you are correct."

"We heard some stuff in Port Alberni," Lucy said. "The locals think they're making fakes."

Yvgeney was charmed by the way the English language fell from her lips, more dimensional than the American word-cascade he was getting used to.

"I tried to get a look inside, but all the windows are high up or down by the water," Wally said. He cupped his ear. "My ear still hurts where that bastard—"

"You haven't told us why you're here." Lucy had a bit of the rascal in her eyes.

"Yeah. What was stolen that brings you here?" Wally asked.

"I was following you, actually," Yvgeney said. "Back in Tacoma, you were the most suspicious character in the room."

"Thank you." Wally beamed. "I am low man on the totem pole of successful sociopaths. The title of Most Suspicious Character in a room with Smith, Brown, and a nefarious-looking, happened-to-be-out-here-camper-dealer from Maine is high praise, indeed."

"Wait a bloody minute," Lucy angled her head, chin up, across the table. "What gives you the right to follow a couple of strangers all the way into another country?"

"It's my holiday, actually."

"Following strangers is your idea of a holiday?"

"It is a long story. Let us say that last week in Tacoma, on my day off from some unpleasant UNESCO business, I attended the auction where I met your companion." He gestured toward Wally. "There I witnessed a crime, perhaps a major art fraud in progress. I investigate stolen art for a living. As you Americans say, art crimes are my beat. I chose to observe your friend's movements through this beautiful Pacific Northwest as a fishing trip for a cultural detective. What I discovered is that you people are bystanders to a criminal enterprise that looks at both of you as a threat. My advice to you is to go back to the United States immediately. I can pursue this investigation after you are safe."

Wally was not nearly as skilled at suspicious character behavior as this odd-accented rescuer seemed to think. He looked into the Russian's weathered face, wrinkled like Belmondo's or Edward James Olmos's. This man that has paid his dues, Wally thought. "So you're an art crime investigator. I bet you've seen some fabulous stuff. Ever chase down stolen furniture?"

"When Hitler swept through Europe he sent teams of art experts into each vanquished region, just behind the first wave. They knew what they were after. Old masters paintings, classical antiquities, and fine furnishings. Looted estates were broken up and dispersed or sold to German collectors. Goering and Hitler actually competed for stolen lots. The best piece of furniture I recovered was from the estate of an Austrian Jew. It was a chest of drawers made by the Frenchman, Charles Boulle. A magnificent object. I recovered it from a museum in Great Britain and returned it to the surviving family. I spent six months on the case. They sold it for 2 million pounds a week after they got it back."

"Ever find anything more modern? Like 20th century?"

"A lot of Viennese furniture by the designer, Hoffmann, was reported missing. Manufactured pieces. Valuable or not, they are hard to trace. I have run into a few chairs. Two weeks ago, in Siberia, I was in a room full of it, stolen from the German thieves by the Russians."

"Joseph Hoffmann, no shit."

"No shit."

"Ever find anything American, like Stickley furniture?"

"No. I am familiar with this recent fascination with the American Arts and Crafts Movement. I watch the goings and comings of a lot of auctions. Hitler would not have stolen it."

"The guy had no vision."

"I agree."

"What's the best painting you ever recovered?" Lucy said.

"I am close to returning a major painting by the artist Gustav Klimt. I was pulled away from that investigation to travel to your Tacoma, Washington. That brings us back to now."

"A Klimt?" Lucy said. "I love his art. So sensual."

"Perhaps I will tell you about it when you two are safely back on your American island. I want you two to go home, *pronto*." He looked at Wally. "Is that the correct word? I am a collector of American folk expressions."

"It works," Wally said. "And I am trying to write a story. Why don't we team up and go back?" Lucy kicked him under the table but he plowed ahead. He'd thought about returning to the mysterious boathouse since he'd fled, but he had no intention of acting alone. "If we could approach that Port Alberni cannery from the water, I bet we could find out what's going on in there." Wally thought, as he spoke, this could be the beginning of a legitimate magazine article, maybe a Pulitzer. A plan formed in his tired mind. "I know the perfect way to become invisible on Barkley Sound." Excited, he laid out a sketchy plan to the table.

Yvgeney asked Wally, "So you think we can motor out into Barkley Sound with fishing gear and check out the building from the water?"

"They certainly won't be expecting us to return."

"I have another idea. I think that you and your lovely English associate should go home this minute and not put yourself in danger that you do not deserve. I am trained for this job. You should go home, resume your lives, and be safe. As quickly as you can. That man was going to kill you both, you know."

"You're just a bloke on vacation, stirring up a conspiracy for sport," countered Lucy. "Don't give us that *duty calls* line. You're out here on guts and a hunch, and so are we. By the way, are you good at self-defense?"

"An expert." He looked into her face.

"Goodie!"

"Three of us would look more normal out in the sound fishing than a single person in a boat," Wally added to his proposal. "And I'm no slouch at self-defense myself."

"Yes, Wally, we noticed in Chemainus," Lucy teased, her eyes on the Russian.

"We can rent some slickers and the gear and boat in Port Alberni and become instantly invisible," Wally said. He was on a roll. "Probably cost us 150 bucks a day, boat included."

"Your vehicle is known to these people," Yvgeney added. "If you insist on this foolhardy venture, we should travel in my car."

Wally said, "I know just the place to stash the van."

Wally parked and locked his Dodge van in a Walmart parking lot south of the diner, careful to cover his load of bark-covered oddities with a blanket.

It was a conspiratorial kinship; three people piled into a black rented Ford on a five-hour journey west to the distant docks of Port Alberni.

Chapter Fourteen

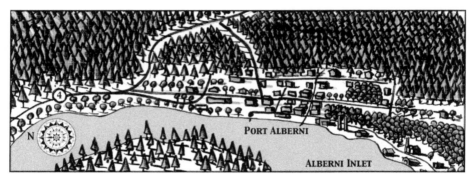

Route Four West, Vancouver Island, British Columbia

Route Four West was a right turn north of Nanaimo. Familiar sights flashed by as the rented Ford retraced the journey to Port Alberni.

Wing World slipped past them on the left. Nobody laughed. A homemade plywood signboard blocked the parking lot entrance: *CLOSED UNTIL FURTHER NOTICE.*

Lucy looked up at the sky above the shuttered roadside attraction. "Are those birds?" she asked, pointing to a flurry of aerial activity above and behind the gardens. Resignation crept across her pretty English face. "I think the butterflies are hearing the sound of freedom."

Yvgeney grimaced. "Let us hope the flock of vultures we are heading into is not so hungry," he said. Neither Lucy nor Wally seemed to hear him.

Late afternoon sunshine sharpened deepening shadows as the westbound Ford crested and descended hills. Lucy pointed out the notch in the cliff leading to the viewing area that had saved their life six hours before.

"That is where you were," Yvgeney said. "I lost sight of your vehicle after the truck hit you. It blinded me with smoke from the brakes as you pulled away. Never noticed that turn off when I passed him and tried to catch up."

"We ducked in the back door to get away from that madman." Lucy grinned. "Chased a couple of sightseers around the parking lot as we slid to a stop."

"Scratched my new sideboard, the son of a bitch," Wally added.

Yvgeney liked the vagabond innocence on the Englishwoman's face as she smiled.

Closer to Port Alberni, the shady canyon of majestic Douglas firs opened up, exposing a vast, denuded plateau bristling with stumps. The Ford ventured deeper into the clear-cut zone as it descended into a valley filled with slash and remains of a thousand-year-old forest. It looked to Yvgeney like a war zone. He bowed his head in dismay.

Lucy said, "Criminal, isn't it?"

Yvgeney said, "I suspect it is like sausage. We like the product, but the process is not pretty."

"The mistake wasn't about cutting the forest," Wally said. "The logging industry broke public relations Rule Number One up here: don't ever let the public see a clear-cut up close, especially on a major tourist highway. This particular clear-cut became a poster-child for environmentalists all over Canada."

A mismatched cluster of lean-tos, plywood shanties, and tents squatted on a ravaged field of tree stumps on the right. "That makeshift village," Wally pointed, "has been hunkered down here for as long as I've been coming here. Er … Yvgeney, would you honk the horn when we pass?" Rolling down the passenger window, Wally gave a thumbs-up to a ragged assembly of young people holding protest signs. The horn blared and the group waved back.

"I suppose you know those people too, Wally," Lucy said and smirked.

"I have some good friends in that group, actually," Wally looked over his shoulder at the rapidly receding village and smiled.

"Oh, come on, Winchester. You can't know everyone on Vancouver Island."

"There's a gal from Camano Island lives here," he said. "Sort of a witchy-woman. Good candidate to be a shaman. She married an Earth-First-type activist from up-island. Really nice guy. Half Indian. They live on an island off the coast of Tofino at the end of this road where it meets the ocean."

"Have I met her?" Lucy asked.

"Before your time, neighbor-girl. Suzan's dad and I were on the Chamber of Commerce together. He invited me up here for his daughter's wedding back in the early 90s. First time I'd been north of Victoria. They live about as far west as you can get and still be in Canada, on a speck of an island plunked down in the Pacific Ocean, so exposed that all its trees grow at a 45-degree angle to the ocean winds. Bad place to be during a tsunami, but otherwise a Pacific Rim Garden of Eden. Natives named it Wickaninnish."

Yvgeney spoke. "In my country, the government would move in and cut any trees they wanted, dam rivers at will, plow down native villages to erect concrete apartments. Anyone protested, they were arrested and sent to the mines in Siberia."

"This guy, Stephen, has been in jail too often to count. Last I heard, he's still facing charges for disrupting a bear hunt."

A colorful but faded tourist sign advertising the good old days indicated the left turn for Port Alberni. Yvgeney engaged the turn signal and asked, "Why would he do such a thing and why was it a crime?"

"There's a new breed of hunters out there, Yvgeney. They hunt from a Zodiac inflatable or a helicopter."

"Platform snipers," Yvgeney said. "That is not hunting. It is target shooting from an armchair."

"Guides get paid for a kill and get to keep the gall bladder to sell to the Koreans for 500 bucks an ounce. The Zodiac hunters, as Stephen tells it, cruise the coast, looking for bears out on the beach hunting salmon in the surf. He tells me they shoot the mothers and leave the cubs to starve. The males, who only come out to the beach at night, rarely end up in the kills."

"Bloody cowards," Lucy said. She stared out the back seat window at clear-cut hills, a sour look on her face.

Yvgeney glanced at the woman over his shoulder, saying, "That is not hunting, that is target practice."

"I was talking about the bears," she said. "Papa bear sends the females out to take the risk. Does his thing after dark when the heat's off."

"Stephen was part of a loosely-knit cadre of coast watchers who kept a constant vigil in the waters along the Canadian shore for that kind of shit," Wally said.

Blue water of the Barkley Sound fjord caught the late afternoon sun and began turning gold. Mill smokestacks appeared through the trees.

Wally hurried through his tale as they approached the waterfront. "One day a boat full of coast watchers showed up at Stephen's dock with a bloody bearskin, head and all. They had come across a beached inflatable 10 miles up the coast and investigated.

They saw skinned remains of a mother bear in the sand and her skin stashed in the poacher's craft, bobbing at the edge of the surf. They saw three hunters farther up the beach, stalking the cubs. Unarmed, they were helpless to intervene. Best they could think of was grab the bearskin and race away with the hunters' prize."

"Why?" Lucy asked.

"Stephen asked the same question. They didn't know, they told him. Said it seemed the right thing to do at the time and asked him for help. He took the skin ashore and advised them to go home."

Lucy said, "That motel we stayed at before is up ahead."

Wally shortened the spaces between his words. "So what does he do with a dead bear? He doesn't know any bear-songs so he and the kids improvise. They take turns making up prayers and tributes and light some candles. Stephen has one more job. The bear. He gassed up his boat and loaded the gutted mother aboard. The answer had come to him during the songs."

Yvgeney pulled the car up to the motel office. He put the rented Ford in park. "What was his answer?" he asked.

"Stephen remembered a guide trip he ran for a filmmaking group. They'd discovered early cave paintings farther up on the west coast of Vancouver Island and hired him to bring up a camera crew. As they filmed, he grabbed a flashlight and wandered into the deep end of the cave. He found a shelf carved into the wall, like an altar. Three ancient skulls sat in the niche."

"Human skulls?" Lucy hadn't left her seat.

"Bear skulls. Old ones. When he remembered the cave, he understood what he had to do."

"He brought the bear carcass to the cave, didn't he?" Lucy said. "Tell me now, we have to register."

"The bear now sits with her ancestors. When Stephen got home, the police were waiting for him at the dock where they arrested him for receiving stolen property. He told the cops he's looking forward to testifying about surf hunting, a story the government doesn't want to be national news. Funny thing, they keep putting off the trial."

Wally's estimate was off by a factor of three. Two-day rental of a Boston Whaler with a big engine and accessories cost 500 dollars, Canadian. The yellow foul weather gear and tackle, another two. Yvgeney winced as he wrote out traveler's checks from his UNESCO account.

They sat on the double beds of the Jolly Fisherman's corner suite and picked through a bucket of chicken. Yvgeney's room was next door. Daylight's last rays illuminated the motel window; the hot pink sunset gave the curtains an eerie glow.

Lucy was antsy. She saw an early evening boat ride as vastly preferable to sitting in a stuffy motel room that held the smell of a thousand previous travelers in the shag carpet. "Hey," she said. "The sun's setting. Let's go fishing."

The sun was three inches over the horizon between the hills as Yvgeney fired up the outboard and motored off with fishing poles and yellow suits into Barkley Sound.

It was a perfect Northwest late-spring evening. Three months of winter rain and gloom were forgotten. The wind was twilight-quiet, and the Boston Whaler cut through a bright crimson mirror toward the northern shore.

Wally actually liked fishing. He cut the bait, frozen herring, in a diagonal technique that he believed was the secret of mooching for salmon. The plan he had described to his boat mates was simple: motor out toward the Pacific Ocean for half an hour before angling right toward the north shore of Barkley Inlet and find the cannery building. As fishermen, he figured, they'd raise no red flags. He pointed to a hazy spit of land in the distance that he guessed would be a good place to begin the search.

"What exactly do we do when we find this place?" Lucy asked, her eyes on Yvgeney as he stood at the center console tiller, throttle wide open.

"That's all I've got," Wally answered over the roar of the motor. "We'll go fishing, see what we can catch. This Russian seems to know what he's doing. First thing, we have to find the place and see what it tells us."

Sharing the back bench with Wally as he fiddled with lines and hooks, Lucy allowed herself a close inspection of the Russian's tight, muscled bum as she scanned the water's edge ahead. He stood feet wide apart for balance as he confidently negotiated the boat over rolling swells and troughs.

"There's a building up ahead at the end of that cove," Lucy said. "Hard to tell if it's the right one from out here. We saw it from the parking lot."

"I was over at the side by the waterline, and I remember how the windows looked," said Wally. He looked up at the two story wood building ahead in the cove. "That's not it. The one we want extends out into the water on piers, like a big boathouse."

Yvgeney squinted into the last of the sunshine and wheeled the boat around expertly in a softly fluid arc, heading west.

Lucy shaded her eyes, peering into nooks and crannies of the undulating northern shore.

A wide cove ahead revealed a substantial building nestled in a forested hill sloping steeply to the water. "That's it," Wally said, looking across the bay with Yvgeney's binoculars. "I recognize the windows high up on the side. Wanna go fishing?"

He set two lines in the water and let out twenty reel-spins of monofilament. Yvgeney held a normal fishing-trolling pattern that gave them a good close passage by the waterside doors for a look-see and not arouse suspicion. The first troll-by told them a lot. The restored cannery had a boathouse with three large, closed doors extending out into the water. Paint peeling on the weathered façade was old, but the vintage building looked in good repair. Modern windows above the bulkhead showed lights burning on the top floor. Below them, older windows filtered greenish fluorescent lighting through drawn shades.

The building slid behind them as Yvgeney steered east around the cove. He was mindful of maintaining the carefree body language of a tourist on vacation.

Lucy, amused and entertained by the fishing experience, was mesmerized by the pink-tinged purple dusk on the Pacific bay. The tip of her pole dove suddenly into the calm water.

"Fantastic!" Lucy squealed, amazed by the power in the salmon's fight. The fish broke the surface 50 feet away, nearly clearing the water with his thrashing tail. He rose again, snapping his head in the air with a surprisingly intelligent, black-bead eye looking at the boat. Then the pole went slack and he was gone.

"Good," she laughed. "I didn't want to catch anything that fought so hard for his life, especially when he looked me in the eye."

Yvgeney said, "We have to go. It will be dark before we reach our dock at Port Alberni."

Wally began to crank and reel his other line. The excitement of the 30-pounder at the boat's edge, even for a second, had fulfilled a little craving in his country soul.

The low throaty rumble of a big, vibrating V-8 engine seemed to come from somewhere behind the boathouse doors and rolled across the water. Invisible in the darkening night, the silent anglers watched as the middle door, moving with a squeaky electric whine, swung wide into the water, revealing a brightly lit interior. Even with his binoculars, Yvgeney could not see the activity inside. The engine's roar intensified; the prow, then the hull of a long, sleek offshore cruiser rumbled across the cove, passing them closely enough for Yvgeney to see two men and a large crate on the back deck. He watched as it disappeared around a point of land into Barkley Sound, toward the Pacific Ocean. In the silence of the warm night, the noise echoed off the distant fjord walls.

The lights of sleepy Port Alberni guided them as Yvgeney aimed his fishing craft back to the dock. A trace of daytime hung over the horizon.

Chapter Fifteen

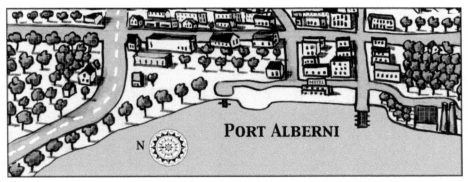

Port Alberni, British Columbia

"I have to get some sleep," Yvgeney announced as they walked to the motel. Four days I have been following you people without a break. I bid you good evening."

He withdrew and closed the door to the corner suite. Through the thin motel wall Wally and Lucy heard the door to the adjacent room open and close.

"That was abrupt."

"He's right, Lucy. We should all get a little sleep. We've had a very full day."

"I'm not ready to settle in just yet. How about one beer and a game of pool at Big John's?"

"People have tried to kill us twice today and you want to go drinking in their town at 11 PM?

"No one knows that we're here, sweetheart." She pecked a kiss on Wally's ear and began to change her shirt. "What bad guys would possibly expect us to come back to Port Alberni? The last they heard, we were in that mural town."

"Chemainus."

"Yeah, that one."

"They'll remember you all right," said Wally. "No short skirts tonight."

Sleep was not an option for Yvgeney, fatigued as he was. He pulled the towels from the bathroom and stuffed them, along with his swim shorts, in his pack. Wearing a dark sweater and a black watch cap, he quietly slipped into the night toward the water.

Big John's Lounge was like a snapshot of the day before. Wally was relieved the three locals Lucy had dazzled earlier were absent. He ordered two dark beers and settled into a booth in the shadow of a monster stuffed king salmon hanging above them on the wall, next to the Labatt Beer neon sign.

Wally sat back and scanned the people in the room, mindful that the log truck in his rear view mirror that morning had probably been driven by somebody from the area, perhaps someone in the tavern. A tired-looking, bleached-blonde-haired woman tended the bar. She brought them two large drafts after chasing another female local who looked like her sister. Cursing in a whiskey-damaged voice, her possible twin left, with the one-finger salute, into the Port Alberni night. The knotty pine room was down to two other customers, Wally noted, and neither of the grizzled, used-up loggers looked capable of mayhem. He sipped the cold beer and sighed.

The Boston Whaler crossed the open water, starlight mixed with reluctant northern twilight vaguely silhouetting the steep land beyond the shore. Pulling his dark cap down, Yvgeney rounded the point of land that led to the cannery's cove and inched his way quietly into the bay. He had seen an entry point when the boat doors opened for the cruiser, but he'd kept it to himself. He slid the two-pronged anchor into the water, silently, without a splash, slowly feeding out the polypropylene rope till he felt the thump of contact a hundred meters below. The slope of the hill behind the building had prepared him for this underwater drop-off close to land.

Dressed in shorts and sporting no self-protection but a fish knife taped to his ankle, he eased himself into the frigid bay.

Cold, cold, shouted his body to his brain, but it came as no surprise. Ten years in the Russian Navy had prepared him for colder shocks. Memories did not help right now. He fought hard to slow his rapid breathing reaction to the icy water. Fifty yards of dark-water swimming took him to the boathouse doors. He drew two deep breaths and dove straight down.

Lucy swirled an inch of beer in the bottom of her glass. She was thinking about the new man who had dropped into her life, wondering if he were married. Her back was to the door, so she was unprepared for Wally's low, frightening curse. "Oh no! I don't believe it. Shit. Lucy, don't turn around."

Her dark eyes widened.

"It's Don Smith. Fuck. He's seen me."

"Good God!" she groaned softly.

Two meters under the cold water's surface, Yvgeney made out a soft glow that marked the bottom of the boathouse door, the murky light suggesting a gap under the frame.

Jack Gunter

Just as I had hoped, the shivering Russian thought as he popped to the surface. He found it amusing that his mind had the patience for short thoughts only as his core temperature plunged. Old training memories made him smile even though his face felt like it was freezing.

After three deep inhalations, he dove down and wiggled under the door, feeling mud and gravel tugging on his chest and belly. With as little noise as possible, he swam toward the light inside, lifting his head above the lapping water. Clearing the saltwater from his eyes, he inhaled diesel-scented air and pulled his shivering body up onto the gangway and caught his breath again. He saw that he was alone, treading water in an empty slip. Barnacled pilings brushed his legs as he pulled himself up onto a loading dock.

Don Smith looked pale. His shoulders sagged as he recognized Wally. Face reddening, Smith slammed a full glass of beer to the counter and approached the booth.

"You've killed us all, you know," he said, squeezing the words through tight lips. He scanned the nearly empty bar, recognizing no one, it seemed, with his dramatic, darting glances. He turned, peering into the darkness outside the front door.

Wally and Lucy sat silently, more embarrassed than frightened, like naughty children caught in a stupid prank. Smith stood at the side of the booth, shaking his head as if to say, "You stupid fool."

"You stupid fool." He sighed. "Do you have any idea what you've done?"

Wally, ignoring his creeping dread, said, "We just wanted an interview."

Smith looked around again. "It's not safe here." He glanced nervously at the dark street outside. "I can't be seen with you. We're all screwed. You really don't have a clue, do you?" His eyes, bloodshot and yellow, looked left and returned to Wally's. "I'll give you the interview of your life, not that it will matter. But not here. Meet me down near the water, at that little park behind the new buildings at the Harbor Quay Marina. You might as well know—"

"We'll see you there in ten minutes," Wally promised, wishing he had a pen and a notebook.

Smith disappeared into the night.

Yvgeney dried himself with two white lab coats. He walked slowly, searching for motion detectors, lasers, a microphone, or any thing else that might betray his incursion. He carefully noted the floor as he entered the building. If Yvgeney's only question had been, "Show me a sign that I am not wasting my time here," the floor would have told him to go ahead, because it was fireproof. Unstrapping the knife at his ankle, he scraped a square of the flat black surface into powder and rubbed it onto his fingertips with his thumb. He felt the deadness, the lack of mineral or metal in the dust. The material was quiet on his fingers, neutral like cheese. The Russian word *karbon* popped into his mind. *A graphite floor!* He understood instantly. They must use a lot of flammables here, he concluded silently. Why would anyone in Port Alberni need a fire-proof floor?

He saw a wall covered with stringed instruments. Violins, a cello, and a couple of oddly familiar 16th century guitar bodies hung on wall hooks above an elaborate craftsman's bench surrounded by fine woodworker's hand tools. A *thump* echoed from a room to the right. Yvgeney stopped and tried to soften his breathing. There were no more noises. He padded over to the bench. A flitch of fiddleback maple, held horizontally with an antique handmade vise, lay on the table. The instruments were beautifully crafted by a master's hand. Violins hanging on the wall were in various stages of construction. It looked like a series of tests.

Old stringed instruments were one of his interests, and Yvgeney realized he had seen this shape on display at the Ashmolean Conservatory in London. The museum description had been vague, crediting the school of Stradivarius. It was a parlor guitar, narrow at the hip, with an elegant neck and intricate ivory inlay.

Yvgeney realized such a rare shape hanging above a workman's bench was odd. Only two of the original Stradivarius guitars were known to exist. The value was untested in the market because none had ever surfaced for sale. Five million dollars for the first one on the market? He'd argued about the estimate with a group of old instrument collectors at a cocktail party in The Hague. The experts had concluded that the price could be much higher in the right auction. Here were three, half finished, hanging from hooks in the wall in the basement lab of a Canadian craft shop.

The function of this hidden workshop was becoming clear. Other areas in the chamber had works in progress, too. The hairs on his neck and arms rose. Old instincts boosted his blood pressure.

The room was a furniture maker's dream. A quick inventory included planers, routers, table saws and workbenches studded with very old hand tools and clamps. An assortment of wide-board lumber stood on end against the wall.

He saw a tin-walled chamber, probably used for fuming and seasoning large objects. A wide range of compressed gas tanks and vats of corrosive chemicals occupied an entire wall.

Through the open door of the fuming box he could see another Chippendale piece, a tea table, supported by gentle cabriole legs and dramatic ball-and-claw feet. It was unfinished, but the mahogany was dark and rich with the patina of 300 years. A series of hoses linked the box with an array of valves and gauges.

Five unmarked doors lead into chambers yet unknown.

"Hello."

Yvgeney froze at the voice.

"What do you do here?" The questioner was a bald, overweight older man in rumpled pajamas, standing to the side of a newly opened door. His accent sounded Slavic.

"I am here to repair the compressor." Yvgeney scrambled for time.

"In your underwear? At two in the morning?" The weathered face showed alarm. "I will call Claus now." The man backed away from the open door, retreating. Yvgeney spun and dashed out to the boat slips. There was no hesitation in his practiced tactical exit. He grabbed a breath and dove into the water, heading for the crawlspace under the boathouse door and Barkley Sound beyond. He dove on a diagonal line toward a spot 10 feet under the waterline where he expected to find the space between the ocean bottom and the boathouse door. His fingers felt the slippery submerged wood as he dove, scrambling downward till he felt the bottom edge. Panic. The backs of his arms brushed against the rounded stones of the Barkley Sound bottom a few inches under the door. Salt water stung his eyes, straining for a glimmer of ambient light. His last deep breath burned in his lungs. This door was different from his entrance target, a few meters to the left. There was no gap a man could swim through—six inches at most. He used the grip on the door bottom to pull his frigid body across to the right, frantically feeling the floor beneath to gauge the empty space he needed to squeeze through to freedom. He pulled his body down, stuck his feet under the door and prepared to propel himself underneath it. He pulled with his arms as his hips and back thrust horizontally into the cove beyond, his buttocks brushing the slimy bottom. He tucked in his elbows and pulled again. His chest was on fire, compressed by the narrow opening. Progress stopped. His upper body didn't quite fit. His arms were pinned against his shoulders. He had no more leverage.

He heard gunfire, muffled by the water, imagined bullets pinging on the surface, streaking toward him. There was no going back to the inside to surface and breathe.

He expelled the remaining oxygen from his lungs and pushed, a last fierce thrust, and felt his upper torso surge into the dark, empty water on the other side.

Stars lit the surface as he burst through and sucked in a welcome gallon of Canadian air. The fishing boat bobbed nearby. Lights blinked on in the previously darkened cannery as he started the Evinrude and opened the throttle wide.

As his boat rounded the rocky point that defined the cove, Yvgeney saw searchlights and flashlight beams criss-crossing the surface by the boathouse doors.

Wally and Lucy walked through the dark streets of Port Alberni toward the dockside park. Wally carried a pen and paper borrowed from the barmaid. They looked equally ill at ease and were silent as they approached a grove of trees illuminated by the evening starlight shimmer of Barkley Sound.

A lamp post by the marina entrance cast strong shadows as its yellow light outlined the cedar trees and picnic tables and trashcans of the shoreline park. Smith was nowhere to be seen. Out across the water, the repetitive drone of a diesel engine suggested someone was awake and working in the chilly Canadian night. Little waves made slapping sounds against the jumbled shore boulders.

"I think he buggered out," said Lucy, uncomfortable in the eerie stillness.

She stopped in mid-sentence when she saw a body beyond the trashcan. Lucy jumped, her toes leaving the loops of her sandals. "Jesus Christ." Involuntarily, she bolted and was almost to the motel when Wally caught up with her.

"Lucy, Lucy!" he wheezed, grabbing her by the arm from behind.

Her eyes were ablaze with panic. "He's dead! Smith is dead!" she shrieked. "What the hell have you gotten us into?"

"Whaddaya mean, he's dead?"

"Smith. He was lying by the trashcan. I saw his body!"

"Fuck."

"We have to wake up Yvgeney. We need him. I want to get out of this place tonight!"

"Let's get back to the room, Lucy. Get out of sight before someone sees us out here." Grabbing her arm, he pulled her through the door of the motel room.

Wally looked for evidence their room had been entered. He found none. They closed the door and Lucy started grabbing clothes and stuffing them into her backpack.

"Hey, slow down." Wally held her shoulders firmly, his voice friendly. "Tell me what you saw."

"He was dead," Lucy said, gulping her words, her flight instinct calming in his firm embrace.

"Are you sure he was dead? Was it really Smith?"

"It was dark, but I saw his face in the light from the dock. The side of his head was all bashed in. I recognized his clothing from the bar. It was Smith, I'm sure."

"We can't leave tonight. We'll be an obvious target at three in the morning. They don't know that we're here, do they? Did you see anyone else? Did they see you?"

"I dunno, I was running. I didn't see anyone else. We've got to wake up Yvgeney."

"Let him sleep. We're all right if we stay out of sight until other people start moving around."

"But he knows self-defense," Lucy pleaded.

"I can protect us, don't worry," Wally said, raising his chin. She turned away to avoid further discussion.

Later, Lucy crept out of her bed as quietly as she could. Silently, she opened the door and looked out at the glowing pre-dawn sky. No movements save some shore birds. No noises but their calls. She slipped out and knocked softly on the door to Unit 128. No answer. She knocked again to no avail. Suddenly frightened again, she stepped back to her door and went back in.

Yvgeney was cautious as he entered his room. Everything was quiet, his amateur allies tucked safely in their room. He had decided on his dark boat ride back to the Port Alberni shore that all three were leaving at the crack of dawn.

Chapter Sixteen

Port Alberni, British Columbia

A knock on the door of Unit 126 brought Lucy and Wally upright in their beds. The knocking began again.

"Wake up. Wake up, it is I, Yvgeney."

Lucy, sobbing, jumped up to let him in, throwing her arms around the surprised Russian.

"We are leaving," Yvgeney said with military certainty. "Pack your things. We have to drive out of here now. You should not be here. Neither should I."

"Sign me up," said Wally, also eager to depart. He noticed how reluctant Lucy was to relax her embrace. He looked at his watch as they marched toward the car. It was 6:30.

Morning fog obscured the water at the shoreline. The seagulls on the fishing dock were silent. Reaching the dew-covered Ford, Yvgeney saw a disturbance in the even blanket of condensation on the hood. Finger marks were visible as swipes of darker finish on the edge of the hood where the latch met the grill.

"Get behind that trash collector," he ordered his companions, directing them to a half-filled dumpster several feet away. Neither argued. Wet leaves brushed their backs as they stood behind the metal container watching Yvgeney work. Dimly visible in the thickening fog, he opened the door carefully to pull the hood latch. He inspected the widening crack as the hood was opened up, looking for a trip wire. Satisfied, he lifted the lid, wincing at the sound of creaking metal, and peered at the engine inside.

Yvgeney shook his head he looked up slowly, searching for movement in the fog. He ran to the dumpster: "We have to get to the boat. They have cut the battery wires. Bring your bags. Now!"

There was no resistance to his leadership.

"Now," ordered Yvgeney. "We are in great danger."

As they climbed into the Boston Whaler, gunfire pierced the fog. A piece of the wooden dock exploded, sending chips into the boat. Yvgeney pushed the start button. The still-warm outboard motor roared to life. Wally tossed off the line.

"Keep your heads down," Yvgeney ordered, as brackish water next to the boat erupted.

Screaming at full rpm, the craft leapt into the dense white blanket through the choppy water. He glanced back and saw three figures at the dock climbing into another craft. Over the roar of the outboard motor, he could not hear the other engine's rumble filling the harbor behind as they fled.

Yvgeney was grateful for the design of the fishing boat they'd rented the day before. A spare fiberglass shell, flat bottomed, with a 100-horsepower Evinrude clamped firmly on the stern, it was the smartest boat in the water when the visibility got low. A six-inch draft rendered it virtually unsinkable. When in the Russian Navy, he'd liked this boat and its handling the first time he drove it. As they hit 25 knots into a blank white wall, he knew that with the flat bottom, the only thing that would stop them in their flight would be the shoreline or the side of another vessel.

"Tell me about this inlet, Wally," he said. "We have to do some navigation soon. There is someone out there behind us."

"I think it's pretty much a straight shot out to the ocean," Wally yelled above the roar of the outboard. "There's a bunch of islands and rocks ahead. Hey, I know a family that lives on an island just up the coast. The people I told you about. They could help us."

With waves spanking the bottom in a soft white invisible world, they planned as they sped blindly toward the Pacific Ocean.

The white morning blanket thinned to a patch of misty blue sky. Ragged hills appeared above the fogbound shore. Clear-cut patches dotted the northern elevations to their right. "Like stubble on a Monday-morning chin." Wally observed aloud. Neither Lucy nor Yvgeney answered. Timbered slopes visible on either side told him that even fog-blind, Yvgeney had managed to keep their bouncing boat in the safe, deep middle of the Canadian fjord.

Suddenly, following the sound of muffled gunfire, a bullet skipped across the surface like a wicked hand-thrown stone. From the bank of white behind them a dark shape with three silhouetted heads emerged. Yvgeney cranked the throttle forward.

"Get down, you two," he commanded. "I think this is a fox hunt and we are the fox. Wally, get your bearings while we can still see the outline of the shore."

Wally popped his head up, glancing at the hills on both sides, trying to recall the inlet's wiggles and little doglegs from his fishing days. "Head that way," he shouted, pointing slightly right. "Closer to the north shore. There's a tight channel by the headland that we can run at high tide. Maybe we can give them the slip there."

Yvgeney had not heard the American phrase, *give them the slip*, before, but it sounded like a better plan than he had. The thick bank of fog near the shoreline began to swallow them again.

A finger-size crescent of sheeting in the bow screeched, peeled away in a ragged curl. "Keep down," Yvgeney said again, knowing that the thin shell was no protection against a high-powered slug. As the Boston Whaler entered the white wall of morning overcast and disappeared once more, Lucy rose up on her knees and flashed her breasts at her pursuers. The bright mist swallowed them up.

Moving cautiously near the shore in near-zero visibility, Yvgeney cursed as a breaking swell pushed the boat into a barnacle-covered boulder. The crunching sound of crumbling exoskeletons reverberated through the fiberglass skin. Wally reached out and pushed the vessel free.

"We have to find a place to hide before the fog burns off," Yvgeney yelled. "Stay low, Lucy, damn it. Wally, where is this island of yours?"

"Once we get to the open ocean, it's ten miles up the coast," Wally yelled back. His words sounded hollow in the canyon of churning surf.

Yvgeney looked down at the pair of five-gallon gas cans that fed the outboard. "We have two hours of fuel at full throttle," he reported. "Do you think that's enough?"

"I guess we'll find out," Wally said, calling up the shape of Barkley Sound from the tattered maps he'd used as a fisherman many years earlier.

As the full-tilt motor pulled them out of the dense soup, Lucy felt sunlight warm her head and back. Blue sky fought for dominance above and won, giving way to a 10-mile vista of open water and a line of dark, surf-washed shoreline toward the north.

"We are the ducks sitting. We have to get past that point of land before we are seen," Yvgeney said, gesturing to a tree-covered spit 500 yards ahead. A row of rounded rolling ocean swells signaled a big change in the water surface beyond the rocks.

The little boat wallowed as the Pacific Ocean surged in repeatedly through the passageway. Guano-stained basalt boulders held their shoulders solid to the crashing surf, soaking the passengers in cold, briny spray. A huge swell pushed them close to a barn-sized rock. Yvgeney goosed the outboard and pulled the craft to the left toward another swell 20 yards ahead. He cut diagonally across the face, rounding the rolling wave as it curled into surf behind them and swept across the rocks. A different world lay ahead: the vastness of the North Pacific opened up around them as they skated across the shoulders of mountainous swells and slid into the deep valleys between.

Lucy peered behind them, looking for signs of their hunters, seeing nothing but crashing waves and dark specks of land.

Wally pointed off to the north. "About nine more miles, almost there," he said.

Lucy found herself somewhere between Zen heaven and Zen hell. What had started out as a three-day lark had morphed into a grim, yet exhilarating ordeal. She studied the craggy face of the stranger who'd popped into her life and perhaps saved it. A small scar on the left side of his sparsely stubbled chin intrigued her. She filed the observation away.

Wally's mind returned to his conversation with Smith at the Port Alberni bar. *What was the message Smith had thought so important he died for the privilege of the telling?* He tried to analyze their encounter. *He seemed to think it was amazing that I didn't know something. Something that should have been obvious to me. Something that he thought was amusing somehow. Something important enough to be murdered for. It must have to do with the auction in Tacoma. That's the only connection we have. Is the table I bought a fake? That's no big deal, it only cost 300 bucks. No one would get killed over a 300 dollar table. Yvgeney was at the auction, but Smith had no way of knowing that we'd teamed up. What did Smith think was so funny?*
The craggy North American headlands gave way to a long sandy beach that stretched as far north as he could see.

Yvgeney could think about Lucy's breasts because the boat handling did not require his full attention. His tactical midbrain was crunching all the available data, leaving him time to savor gentler pleasures.

His conscious thoughts took him back to the edge of a bank of fog. He was tickled by the British woman's act of defiance, stupid as it was in a gunfight. Her strong English nose and wind-blown curly hair had the quirky grace of a Lampecka painting. She'd stood there like Joan of Arc, shoulders back in childish insubordination, her chest jutting forward in a feminine "Fuck you!" to her oppressors. Of course it had been a foolish gesture that could have gotten her killed, but as he crested another broad Pacific Ocean swell, he found himself smiling.

Chapter Seventeen

Wickaninnish Island, British Columbia

Wickaninnish Island, half a mile long and a couple of hundred yards wide, appeared as a dark smudge on the horizon. It sat alone in the Pacific Ocean. Across an inlet, a group of buildings on the shore of another island looked like a village to Yvgeney. He asked Wally about it.

"That's Tofino over to the right," Wally stood up and pointed to distant docks and increased boat traffic ahead. "It's Canada's mecca for the New Age culture. One of those high energy spots that the TM people flock to."

"What is TM?"

"Transcendental meditation, Yvgeney." Lucy said. "It's a trance-like—"

"I know of this meditation," Yvgeney cut her off. "I lived with a Buryat shaman."

The sighting of the islands was a great relief to Yvgeney, who hadn't mentioned his fear about the fuel supply to his companions. As the flat-bottomed fishing boat cruised along the inside channel, a dock was visible off the tree-filled island shoreline. Two Zodiac inflatables floated on the near side. On the far side, a 30-foot vintage mail boat with a brightly painted canvas sunshade covering the rear deck stood at anchor. Yvgeney threaded his craft through the buoys and floats to reach a clear part of the dock.

Lucy tied it off and the trio climbed gratefully onto solid land.

At the forest edge two barefoot children appeared, one a little blond girl in a bathing suit, the other a pre-teen boy wearing shorts. They approached the disembarking visitors cautiously, but without hesitation, displaying neither fear nor trust.

"Hi, Ethan. Hello, Shannon. It's me, Wally, remember? Last summer we went whale watching with your dad."

The children didn't move.

Wally asked, "Where are Stephan and Suzanne? Do you guys still have the train set I gave you last year?"

Recognition crossed the young faces. "We saw orcas yesterday," the younger one exclaimed.

"Dad's up in the boat shop," Ethan said. "Mum's away, painting." The children turned their backs, trusting the man who gave them the trains, and led the visitors up a well-used path.

Ten thousand years of evolution on this tiny bit of land had produced a miniature old-growth preserve. Wally patted gnarly windswept trunks, bent toward shore like frozen cartoon trees as he walked the narrow passage. "Hello, old guys," he said. He imagined the constant ocean storms and wild conditions that favored the lowest profile. Walking like a giant through the gnome-sized forest of thousand-year-old cedar and Douglas fir, he spotted a familiar structure.

At the back of a hand-hewn house perched near a cliff, a half-naked man met them by the door. His curly hair was greying at the temples. He was shirtless, wearing a pair of shorts and boots. Blue eyes were set deep in his face above his prominent nose and clean-shaven jaw. "Hello, Wally, nice to see you." He spoke in a rich, low voice with Canadian roots.

"Hello, Stephen," Wally said. "You have no idea how nice it is to see you." He introduced his haggard companions as the tall man invited them in to get comfortable and have something warm to drink.

Inside, the fragrance of wood and herbs mingled with cool salt air pouring in the open windows. Wally looked around at one of his favorite interiors. It was a palace of hand-built delights. A sweeping staircase connected to a balcony whose railings seemed to grow from the floorboards like a Rousseau jungle of knots and intertwining limbs.

"This place is wonderful," Lucy said.

Wally's eyes danced around the sunlit room and rested on a large burl tabletop supported by a lyrical base of rusted steel. Tall-backed chairs in the manner of Frank Lloyd Wright nested around it, their square, tall spindles showing the wobbly highlights of a hand chisel on their sides. Stout, nut-brown bookcases lined an alcove to the rear. The silvery aluminum knuckles of a Warren Macarthur lounge chair, another Victoria bargain, added a Machine Age bubble to the warm wood interior.

Pink sunset colors shone through 10-square-foot front windows and backlit Wally's windblown hair as he recited the last day's events to Stephen and his family.

While Lucy snoozed on a Thomas Molesworth settee, Yvgeney excused himself to check on the boat and wander the perimeter.

"I can carry you over to Tofino," Stephen said. "You can take the Suburban and leave it in Chemainus when you get there. I can pick it up next week."

"Where's Suzanne?" Wally's fatigue was closing the window of his attention.

"She's working on a painting," Stephen said.

Yvgeney appeared at the back door. "They're here," he said, out of breath. "At the dock."

"How did they find us?" Wally asked, quickly waking up.

"They must have put a homing beacon on the fishing boat," said Yvgeney. "Is there another way off this island?"

"I've got another Zodiac in the ocean-side cove. Follow me," Stephen shouted, herding his two children down to the ocean shore where an inflatable offshore sport boat bobbed soundlessly in the shallows, tethered to a dry land stake. The outboard roared alive as dark shapes on the cliff-top opened fire. The Zodiac lurched forward as a familiar fountain of pings and pops speckled the surf around them.

The boat bounced hard as it planed across the three-foot swells. The six passengers held on tightly as evening twilight swallowed up their view. Five miles out to the north, Stephen throttled down. A back wave lifted the inflatable and let it go as the boat floated to a stop.

"Have we lost them?" Lucy asked peering into the gloom.

Stephen said, "Whoever's following you couldn't estimate our heading in this light. By the time they reached their boat and rounded the island we were out of sight. I think you can relax. I know of a cave up the coast where we can go for a night's sleep."

A cool blanket of air settled on the water as the last crescent of the sun winked out. Lucy tried to suppress a shiver, then shook violently for a few seconds. Yvgeney slid closer beside her, opened his heavy jacket to her. "I hope your partner doesn't mind if I keep you warm," he said. He looked to the stern at Wally, who seemed nonplussed by the protective gesture.

"Wally is not my partner," Lucy said, giggling. "He's my neighbor." She looked up into Yvgeney's face. "Did you think that Wally and I are?"

"Aren't you? You sleep in the same room."

"Oh my heavens, no. Wally has a girlfriend back on Camano Island. We're all friends. Trust me, Yvgeney. I'm only on this trip because I was bored and it sounded like fun." She leaned closer as his arm cradled her in a pocket of quilted insulation but changed her mind and sat up, away from his cozy coat. "Are you married? I apologize. Please excuse me. I was so cold. It's been such a terrifying day."

"I'm not married," Yvgeney said, again offering her the protective embrace of his coat. She climbed back in. The Russian's heartbeat thumped in her ear as he gathered her deeper. Tension floated off her shoulders; she fought the urge to purr. Turning toward him, she draped one arm across his denim shirt and buried her face against his chest. A strong but not disagreeable odor seemed to fit him. His muscular torso was a discovery. Nice six-pack was a thought she chased away. The events of the past 24 hours—the kidnapping attempt at bat- and gun-point, the runaway logging truck, seeing Smith's body—all seemed a million miles away. "I've known you less than 20 hours, Mr. Russian Hero, and already I'm feeling you up." She scolded herself, reluctantly dragged her hand off his solar plexus and looked up at him. "Who are you, really? And what are you doing in my movie?"

Yvgeney tilted his lined, weathered face toward hers. Despite herself, she tilted her face, preparing for a kiss. He spoke instead. "I like the phrase, in my movie." His warm breath eddied in the pocket created by his arm. To Lucy it smelled of wheat grass.

"My hobby is cataloging interesting American phrases. I collect them. Do you mind if I add your words to my database? Where does it come from? A film? A TV character?"

Lucy smiled at the chivalry of such an unusual request. "You're an odd duck," she said to his chin, looking up, liking him more. "It's a state of awareness, a metaphor that allows a person to observe themselves on their passage through time. It's a trick I learned from a self-help book. It tells you that every person lives inside the movie of his or her personal perceptions. They write, direct, produce the movie of their lives, and they provide the audio. They allow other people in and out of their movie as actors. If they're smart or lucky they can control the script of their movie. They resent it when other movies want to tell them how to fix the one they're in." She lifted her chin nearer his. "Yesterday you crashed into my movie with an aluminum cricket bat. Thank you, by the way. Who are you? Why were you really following us?"

The breeze at his back pushed curly dark hair into his eyes. "In my movie I need a hat," he said, reaching down into his coat with his free hand and extracting his black watch cap. "I told you already. I work for the United Nations. I investigate crimes against cultural property."

"You've given me no new information. What are you doing on this side of the world? Wally's no international man of mystery, believe me."

"Technically, I am on holiday."

Lucy shook her head.

"All right, I was sent here, to Tacoma actually, to open up and search the contents of hundreds of metal drums shipped from Korea."

"Sounds like a job for the Coast Guard, not the UN. What were you searching for? Dirty bombs?" Her hand fought her urge to rub his taut chest muscles.

"The drums were filled with the most foul substance in the universe. I still smell it on my fingertips if I rub my nose."

"Does this have something to do with the Republican Party?"

"I work in the United Nations, remember? I have been up to my neck in political rhetoric. Trust me, that smells more like the offerings of a bull. What is the most disgusting thing you can think of?"

"You had to sort through barrels of Courtney Love's *knickers*? You poor baby."

"Courtney Love?" he said. "I do not know the name."

"She's a singer, part of the old Grunge movement in Seattle. Well-known for her potty mouth."

"Potty mouth? Grunge? These are wonderful American words. What do they mean?"

"Potty mouth, chamber pot. Do the math. Grunge describes a musical sub-category where a state of filth and unkemptness and the lack of interest in personal appearance was part of the band's message. Music for outcasts. Very popular a few years back." She raised her free arm and pointed aft toward Wally, sitting with Stephen next to the outboard. Wally noticed and waved enthusiastically, giving the thumbs-up. "Wally," she continued, "could be a trend-setter in the Grunge movement if he could play the guitar."

"Grunge," Yvgeney said.

"Grunge."

"Grunge," Yvgeney said again. "I like it. It is a good word to find. Even the saying of it sounds dirty."

He looked back at Wally in the stern, barely visible in the last light of a very long day. "Grunge," he shouted into the roar of the Evinrude. Wally smiled and waved back.

"You're the king of all sloppy men, Wally!" Lucy shouted, her voice carried by the wind at her back. "Grunge hero!"

Wally beamed.

"It was cod skins in the drums."

Now it was Lucy's turn to be confused. She knew the definition of the Old English word codpiece and the possibilities were frightening.

"The skin of the fish, cod. This shipment of barrels arrived on a freighter two weeks ago in the port of Tacoma. At that time I was in Siberia, researching Austrian masterpieces in the cozy basement of a city picture gallery."

"Who on earth would want all those fish skins?"

"Fertilizer factories, cat food canners, people who really hated their neighbors, or perhaps people who did not want the containers inspected."

"Smugglers?"

"The drums were metal—difficult to x-ray. The smell was astonishing. The customs inspectors ran the unopened barrels in front of a magnetometer, hoping to avoid any more open containers. Well, they found something. From under a half-meter of gore they extracted a stone carving of two figures embracing. No one in the customs office knew what to do. They called in art experts from Seattle. One identified the sculpture as resembling the Brancusi artwork called *The Kiss*. Brancusi was a Rumanian sculptor—"

"I know the bloke. I'm a student of style, sir."

"Forgive me, I do not know you yet. Well, my bosses in UNESCO told me to pack my bags and fly to Tacoma. That is how I found myself in the United States, opening 150 barrels of the devil's own sputum, unpeeling stacks of clotted flesh, layered like lasagna—*lasagna putrefaciento*.

"There was nothing more to be found, of course. The original stone sculpture was hosed off and measured. Checking my UNESCO database, I found the dimensions did not match any Brancusi version of *The Kiss*, stolen or not. It was a copy." He brought his free right hand over to her face. "Want to experience the odor of cod?"

Lucy buried her face in his shirt, shaking her head, no, then stopped. "Yes, Yvgeney." She reached out and brought the fingers to her nose, inhaling deeply. The scent of decay filled her sinuses. "Welcome to America. I still don't know why you're way up here. What does Wally have to do with this? He's a flippin' idiot. A brilliant one, I think, but he's no threat to any cultural property unless it has oak legs and belongs to your grandma, and then you'd better watch out. I have one more question."

"Ask away."

"Do you presently have a girlfriend?"

Yvgeney pulled her closer. He said, "Maybe."

Wally sat in quiet thought, oblivious to the sound of the motor. He was thinking of Rae. Their relationship was fairly new, about a year now, and it was entering an interesting phase. She was nice enough, cute enough, with the long blonde hair and high cheekbones of a Nordic princess. She had a big heart, she was passionate, and she was smart. She was even an artist, a photographer who had earned a reputation in the Northwest. She liked antiques. A little. There was the rub. She was not good on the road, preferring the security of a comfortable home and a nine-by-five job. They'd made some trips together, sure, but she didn't have the Don Quixote impractical idealism required for serious pickers. Paying attention to every windmill you pass when you're on the road, even the rumors of one, was not her idea of a good time.

Wally had never found a female road partner who shared his passion for the false starts, uncertainties, dead ends, sheer luck, follow-through, and guts that lead to a big score. He knew the other pickers, reptiles all, had the same problem with their partners.

Then he thought about the look in her eyes when they made love. He remembered the quickening of his pulse he always felt when he approached her front door. He pictured candlelight dinners in San Francisco, tired after a day of museum strolls, as he listened to her insights into photography and art and time and the illusion of permanence.

He decided he missed her a great deal and concluded that it was a good thing she said no to this particular trip. If Rae had said yes back in the hot tub when I asked her to come up here, he thought, and she ended up out here in the Pacific-fucking Ocean getting shot at by crazies, she'd never get in the van with me again.

"Why, again, were you following us?" Lucy asked Yvgeney.

"It was an accident. Back in Tacoma I attended the auction that brought us together—just as a tourist—to watch a five million dollar desk get sold. I gave 50 dollars to a young man at the door, but it was worth it in entertainment value. The auction made no sense. The consignor, the man you knew as Smith, bought back the first lot himself. Then your friend, Wally, walked away with a valuable table for *peanuts*. Then the auctioneer tried to set a five million dollar desk on fire."

Yvgeney looked serious. "I am an investigator. There was some art crime taking place, but I could not figure out what it was. It was time for my holiday. I was hooked by the mystery."

Lucy said, "I don't think American fishermen say that, Yvgeney."

"My slang collection is a work in progress."

"Wally looked at the whole thing as a joke. He's laughed about that auction ever since he came back. He told me he finally beat his friend Brown at his own game. He says he's writing a magazine article. Maybe he will, though I've never seen him write anything but eBay descriptions. I think the idea to interview Smith was just an excuse for him to come north and mess with the network he has on Vancouver Island. You'd be amazed at the people he knows here. I believe he knows everyone on this bloody island. *So far I'm right.*"

Yvgeney said, "I did not know how your friend fit into this, I just knew he was involved. Follow the money. I granted myself three days of holiday time to observe the Grunge master." He flashed Wally the split-finger peace sign he'd observed in the movie about the Woodstock Music Festival. Wally returned it. Yvgeney said, "When I watched him at the cannery—"

"You were there?"

"I enjoyed watching you dip your French fries in vinegar on the ferry crossing."

"Did you watch me in the shower at that kitchenette cabin near Campbell River?"

"No."

"If you play your cards right, you might get a second chance." Lucy said. She felt his right hand cover hers resting on his chest.

Yvgeney sat up, releasing her fingers. He said, "My antenna was accurate, Lucy. Wally, unwitting or not, has exposed a nest of the hornet. There are people on this island, bad people, who do not want any public attention. We have international agencies like Interpol who deal with the crime that I think I have discovered. My highest calling now is to help you and your friend get back to the United States safely. Especially you."

"I think I'm lucky you came to rescue us. Were you an officer in the Russian Army? I'm impressed by the way you take charge." She pressed her head deeper into his side.

"I was in the navy. I was an information officer on minesweepers that patrolled the Artic Ocean. My job was to listen to American *chatter*. Most of the broadcasts we could decipher were North American television shows. I listened to many news programs, but I learned much more about the West by listening to, what is the word? Situation comedies? Like *The Simpsons* and *Cheers* and *Saved by the Bell*. I only received the audio, but that told me a lot about how Americans think. The boys on one ship held endless discussions about what that woman on *Baywatch*, C. J. Parker, looked like."

"Pamela Anderson."

"Excuse me?"

"Pamela Anderson played C. J. She has blonde hair and she's a knockout."

"I know. I have looked her up on the Internet. *The Simpsons* taught me the most about everyday life in America. Many of my intelligence recommendations were based on information gleaned from that broadcast."

"You based Russian intelligence reports on the plots of a cartoon?"

"*The Simpsons* is a cartoon? Ooops."

Lucy laughed. "Where were you born? What's your sign? What's a nice guy like you doing in a place like this?"

"I know that phrase. W. C. Fields?"

"Humphrey Bogart. When we get back I'm going to take you to the movies."

"To answer the first question, I was born in Moscow, into a family of art dealers. That is one reason I am in the Cultural Properties program. I get to undo many wrongs. Stolen masterpieces are crimes against humanity. I must admit, Lucy, that I have not enjoyed my work much lately."

"That fish-skin business?" Lucy lifted his hand to her nose and inhaled. She kissed a knobby knuckle.

"More than that. It seems that these days, many of the objects I recover for families of the victims have no meaning for the new generations. They end up on an auction block, exchanged for a handful of cash. I sometimes feel more like a ... what is the slang for *whoremaster?*"

"Pimp."

"Pimp. I feel more like a pimp than a hero."

A rocky promontory gave way to the darker emptiness on an inlet ahead. Stephen guided the Zodiac toward a beach shrouded by tall coastal trees. They followed the children as they leaped from the boat and pranced up the trail like deer. Wally looked up at the kids ahead, standing on a flat shelf illuminated by dim light from inside the hill.

Stephen stowed the boat gear and watched the entrance to the little harbor. It was silent except for wind in the cedars at his back and the rhythmic frothing of the surf. No one could find them.

A six-foot crevice in the boulder-strewn hillside opened into a small irregularly shaped chamber. The visitors had watched as the children ducked their heads and scrambled under a low-ceilinged opening, disappearing into a room on the other side. Two years ago I hear about this bear cave and now I'm here, thought Wally looking into the interior of a lantern-lit cavern.

"Scoot under here, you guys, it's all right." Shannon's head poked back out from the constriction. "Don't be afraid, there's lots of rooms inside."

Lucy found the glow of light from under the low passage enticing when she dove in head first behind the smaller child, crawling hands and knees under a thousand tons of stone to enter a tall, narrow underground canyon beyond.

Illuminated by a flickering kerosene flame, the chamber was about 10 feet wide, sharing the floor space with the slowly moving blackness of a stream exiting the room at a low hollow in the subterranean hall. The walls were perpendicular, rising 10 feet to the ceiling dome. The lantern cast a surreal glow on the figures of the children before her. Long shadows preceded them alongside the dark water as they headed for the back of the underground room. The art on the wall commenced there.

Standing alone in the darkness outside the entrance, Yvgeney ran through a mental list of potential strategies for the exit from Vancouver Island toward the safety of the US beyond. It was surprising to encounter a kerosene-lit cavern on the cliff of a rugged unpopulated shoreline halfway to Alaska, but security came first. His curiosity would have to wait. He sat back against a hillside tree trunk next to the opening and waited for Stephen.

"There's no one behind us," Stephen said as he climbed to the flat shelf.

"I imagine we are out of reach for now," Yvgeney agreed.

Stephen, breathing normally despite his sprint from the beach, added, "I know you have some military training. I see and hear it in your manner."

"Soviet Navy, Second Fleet, ten years. Captain, second grade."

"I'll stay out here and make sure we weren't followed," Stephen volunteered. "Go on in." He gestured toward the dim light. "I think you'll enjoy Suzan's work."

Yvgeney felt a hundred questions, but they all involved the logistics of the next day's departure from Vancouver Island. He thanked Stephen for his help and wandered into the cave.

Wally stood near a long petroglyph. It began with line drawings of bison and deer. A reddish pigment mixed with charcoal seemed to have lasted many thousands of years. The line of drawings marched onward like a prehistoric circus parade. Visions of bison and mastodons and hunts and death. Half way to the far end, he could see blue color. It started imperceptibly on the flattened limestone slab. Specks of brilliant cerulean blue appeared on high points, getting gradually denser toward the interior bend of the chamber. Dark smudges of landscape under the light blue sky followed the cerulean flow.

Lucy was 30 feet ahead, gazing at this change in the artwork style farther down the wall. She had stopped in front of a mural featuring animal and human figures and tan square forms that suggested a village nestled on an ocean shore, mountains and a giant ice field at their back. It was clearly the work of a contemporary artist.

As the children disappeared around the corner another voice was audible from deep within an area yet unseen. Wally was struck with the soft transition on the wall from old to new.

Original Finish

The last 20 feet of the first chamber were covered by a brilliant landscape painted in vibrant blues and greens and ochre. Fluffy clouds were painted above the purple-and- white distant peaks. A deep blue-black ocean, waves delineated by white edges, formed the base of this huge tableau, overpainted with beaches and foothills, fields and stadiums and imagined buildings and human activity. Wally walked farther toward the interior, reading the story of another time, painted in a crisp modern hand.

The voices were louder now. Wally and Lucy looked over to see Suzanne Eagleton, paint brush in hand, her children beside her, emerging from a deeper chamber around the corner.

"Hi, Suzan." Wally's smile was tired. "I had no idea you were working on something like this!"

Susan smiled. She wore a blue kerchief over shoulder-length salt-and-pepper hair. Wally smiled, appreciating her friendly face. Her coveralls were spotted with paint.

"This is my friend, Lucy," Wally said. "From England via Camano."

Yvgeney entered. His head bobbed up and down as he took in the brightly painted mural.

"And Yvgeney Ivanchenko. Ivanchenko ... is that correct?" Wally asked.

"That is correct," Yvgeney said.

"This is my friend, Suzan. She's the creator of this incredible project."

Susan smiled again. "I've always wanted to record the story of the struggle to save the land out here," she said. "I didn't want to make a big deal about this work. Actually, it's kind of private. You're the only people, other than my family, who've been in here."

Dropping the wet paintbrush into a jar, she said, "The kids say you're in some kind of trouble."

125

Wally nodded. The memory of the wild boat adventure faded as he looked upon the giant painting.

"Tell me about this amazing thing you're making."

"Well," Susan began, holding Wally's attention for a second longer with her eyes. "Those first six drawings were here when Stephen discovered this cave."

"Is the bear skull altar here?" asked Wally, happy to be in her sphere once more.

"No, Wally, that's way up the coast," the younger child said. "Daddy doesn't tell anyone where that cave is."

"The walls were empty in this end of the cave," Susan said, pointing to the areas beyond the second room. "I gave the original artwork lots of space, then let the wall tell me where to begin, as you can see."

"I tried to tell the story of Vancouver Island in three parts. This room depicts the ancient ways and people. Down around the corner," she nodded over her shoulder, "a second wall tells the story about today ... farther in is the wall I'm on now. It's sort of an allegory about the future."

Years of work covered the large wall. Lucy marveled at the artist's drive that would propel her to the dark and soundless hidden world to form her connection with the earth. She wondered if the motivation of the first artists in similar darkness eight thousand years before was much the same, and she concluded that it probably was.

"How 'bout some hot tea and a futon," Suzan offered. "You look like you've been squeezed through the hinges of hell." Lucy settled alongside Yvgeney onto a down-filled cushion that served as

Susan's bed and living room. Lucy thought she'd never felt a more satisfying softness in her life.

Later, Suzan said, "It sounds like quite a can of worms that you've opened for yourself, Walter Winchester." Yvgeney and Lucy snored soundly on the futon. "I think that Stephen's right to offer the use of the Suburban. No one would recognize you in that rig. You could drive right off the island and onto a ferry. It even has tinted windows. You'd be invisible. You can leave the rented car in Port Alberni and whoever these people are, they'll spend the week beating the bushes up here and you'll be home safe."

Wally sighed involuntarily.

"I've got some things in Chemainus. In my van," he added. "But I think we'll be out of danger by then."

The children had found their own comfortable beds in the familiar recesses of the cave. Suzan cleared away the other futon side and lay with Wally for a minute. She snuggled up behind him and put her arms around his chest in a protective embrace. Wally was instantly asleep.

Chapter Eighteen

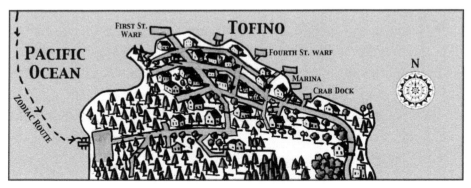

Tofino, British Columbia

"When we get to the town dock, Ethan will jump out and retrieve the Suburban," Stephen said. He was going over the itinerary with his three passengers as they motored toward the entrance to Tofino Harbor. "You three keep your heads down. It'll take me half an hour to get us around the Tofino peninsula to Wickaninnish Point and the picnic area. No one will be out there at eight in the morning. Once you're in the Suburban, you'll be invisible till you reach the border."

Wearing borrowed hats and jackets, Lucy, Yvgeney and Wally leaped ashore, scrambling for the safety of the dark-windowed 80s Suburban, sporting a long front snout and a yellow band along the side. A well-used set of roof racks were bolted to the top. Wally turned the ignition key and a finely tuned motor roared to life.

Serenaded by Canadian Public Radio, they drove east into the hazy sun, reentering the vast landscape of clear-cut stumps and snags. Wally drove, wheeling the borrowed vehicle down the familiar road.

Half an hour into the drive they passed the entrance to Smith's clock shop on the right. All three drew in their breath. As they passed the rest area and headed down to the valley of Port Alberni, Wally allowed himself the luxury of hoping that everything was going to be all right. He had discovered a cell phone hanging out of sight under the radio. He drove one-handed as he fiddled with the calling codes.

Yvgeney and Lucy were deep in a European reminisce: "In our country," remarked the Russian, watching the clear-cut ridge tops roll away, "it is the government who comes in and does whatever it feels like with the land. The people have no voice."

"You sound like you didn't like the Communist government," she said.

"It is easy to love your country but not the idiots who control it," Yvgeney said.

"Amen," said Wally from the front seat. He dialed Rae's number as he drove.

She answered. "Hi, Honey. How are you? I've been worried. You haven't called."

"Just a minute," Wally said. Over his shoulder he said, "Quiet down, you two, I've got Rae on the phone."

Yvgeney looked at Lucy. She winked, and nodded toward Wally.

"I've had an interesting trip," Wally said, his voice low.

"How's Lucy? Are you two behaving?"

"I think she's found a gentleman. An interesting man. He's traveling with us as we speak. In fact, he and she are in the back seat right now. They're chatting like there's no tomorrow."

"I told you, no hitchhikers. You promised. Wait a minute," Rae said. "What do you mean, *back seat*? You left in your Dodge van."

Wally began to explain the mess he was in but Rae interrupted, "Honey, I have some terrible news. Very sad."

"What?" A multitude of horrors ran through Wally's head. My cabin burned down. I missed some Stickley at a Camano garage sale. My Tiffany lamp fell and smashed the shade. The hot tub sprung a leak.

"Wally, I have to call you back. When you rang I had a photo darkening in the developer. I have to tend to it."

"Whaaa. Don't tell me you've got bad news and then hang up."

"Your number is on my phone. Let me call you back."

"Did you spill something on the lamp table I just bought?"

"Gotta go." Wally heard the disconnect.

They drove past a picnic area in an old-growth grove. No one suggested stopping to stretch their legs. Until they got to Camano Island, they all agreed, the dark windows of the Suburban would be their friends. Wing World, open again, its parking lot filled with RVs, zipped by.

Wally's borrowed phone rang, Rae calling back. "Wally?"

"I'm here for you, baby. It's been a tough trip."

"Your friend Ed Brown is dead."

Yvgeney continued talking to Lucy, "When I joined the Russian Navy I carried with me a personal understanding of our Communist bureaucracy and its treachery."

"Did they imprison your family? Send them to the gulag?"

"No, the Communists treated my family well, for some years at least. My father was a prominent art dealer."

"He bought and sold paintings, behind the Iron Curtain? I would think that was a jail-able offense back then."

"The Soviets owned many masterpieces. They needed experts. My father was the best. He specialized in icons. He traveled to London and New York on behalf of the USSR. That is when I became interested in American culture. He took me to London once, while he evaluated an icon called *Kazanskaya*, the Mother of God of Kazan. The most holy icon of all. That is when he ran afoul of the Kremlin."

"What happened?"

Yvgeney took Lucy's hand. He caressed the top of her fingers with gentleness that surprised her, almost bringing a tear. "I will tell you sometime," he said. "It is a long story." Nodding toward the front seat, he said, "Wally is receiving troubling news. We should give him a quiet car."

"Your friend, Brown, is dead, did you hear me?'

"Yeah," Wally said. "There was noise in the car. Ed's dead?"

"A dealer from Olympia called yesterday. Jerry."

"Go on."

"He told me he's been trying to reach you for two days. He said they found Brown face down in a vat of acid early Wednesday morning. Pretty gruesome sight, I imagine. His face was gone, eaten off. The hands were nothing but bones. Still had his wedding ring, Jerry said. The police figure he fell off his balcony above the woodshop and landed face down in the tank. No one's seen Laura, either. The cops don't know what to think, but they're trying to find her. His auction house is shut up tight."

"Good grief," Wally said. They were two miles from the right turn to Victoria, two highway hours south. *They got Ed. Everybody involved with that auction is turning up dead and we're on the list.*

Wally kept his ear on the phone. "Sorry about your friend, Wally," Rae said.

"Thanks." Wally's head was spinning.

"One more thing," Rae said. "A lady from Campbell River called. Said you bought a sideboard. She wanted me to tell you her

131

sister brought over the table and chairs that match. Three lamp tables, too. Does that make sense to you?"

"It certainly does," Wally said.

"Tell me about your trip, Wally."

"It's been a blast. Now I gotta go. Love ya."

Yvgeney was talking softly in the back seat. Wally stared straight ahead, lost in thought as he drove. There was plenty of time on the three-hour drive to Victoria to give his passengers the Tacoma news.

The Suburban reached the T-junction where the road to the safety of the Victoria ferry turned south. Wally said nothing to his mates, glad they were preoccupied, and turned north toward Campbell River, 30 miles up the road.

Yvgeney's sense of orientation said their direction was 180 degrees off. "Are we headed the right way, my friend?" he asked, recognizing the Inside Passage to his right. Tree-filled islands and mainland foothills lay beyond the wide inlet with the snow-capped coastal range beyond. Two log tugs offshore pulled a long log raft. "The water suggests we're heading north."

"I've got one little stop to pick up the rest of a very cool dining room set," Wally said, as if the harrowing last three days didn't matter. "Don't worry, Yvgeney. We're off the radar now. No one in this family we're visiting knows anything about the shit we stepped in out here."

"I don't like it, Wally." Lucy said.

"I agree with Lucy," Yvgeney said. "Our best safety lies in the United States. There are people on this island who want to hurt us. The things I saw when you were sleeping in Port Alberni told me we are dealing with very serious people who have a lot to lose."

Wally ignored Yvgeney's concerns. "It's only 10 more minutes and then we can turn right around. No one will see us. I promise."

"Ten minutes north," Yvgeney said under his breath as he turned a log-legged chair sideways to fit it into the back of the Suburban, now stuffed with rustic furniture.

"That's Wally-math." Lucy was beside him, helping with the insertion. "You'll get used to it. I usually divide any number out of his mouth by three. But this time I should have multiplied. The 10-minute detour took an hour."

Wally slammed the back Suburban door closed, then climbed into the driver's seat, waving back at the smiling Canadian woman as he backed out of her driveway.

"Happy, now?" Lucy asked. She noticed the concern on Wally's face. It was an expression she wasn't used to.

"That nice man down the street was found dead this morning," Wally said as he drove. "Killed himself, she told me. Said they found him hung with his own Iron Man belt. What a shame. Now he's in heaven with Johnny Cash. If it wasn't for old Jack, we wouldn't have found Smith."

Yvgeney frowned.

They passed the refinishing shop on the next block. A hand-lettered *Closed* sign was nailed to the door. Wally asked if he could stop and leave a note of condolence to the next of kin with his phone number in case they needed help with the estate. He was shouted down by both his companions. He didn't argue as he drove south.

133

Chapter Nineteen

Route 1-A to Victoria, British Columbia

The Suburban's tinted windows made the afternoon overcast appear darker. At Yvgeney's suggestion, they took turns reciting their individual experiences during the last three days to see if they could make some sense of their dilemma.

Lucy told Yvgeney about the meeting with Smith and seeing his body by the shore.

Yvgeney told Lucy and Wally about his midnight swim and the forgery laboratory he thought he had found. "I am not the police," he explained. "There are other authorities that will be brought to bear. I have limited resources and I am tied to the hip with two amateurs." Eye-to-eye with Lucy, he said, "I cannot do my job and worry about danger to civilians, especially one that I find so intriguing."

"I agree. Murdered people are a job for the police, not NATO paper pushers or make-believe magazine writers," Lucy said, arching her back in a seductive stretch. "The faster we're on Camano Island, the happier I'll be."

"Ed Brown is dead," Wally said during a quiet moment.

"The auctioneer?" Yvgeney said.

"Yeah, the auctioneer. They found him in a vat of acid in his shop—half dissolved."

"Yech."

"Yeah, and his wife is missing. Rae told me when we were on the phone, but I haven't found the time to tell you till now."

"The auctioneer dead, and Smith, and some very serious attempts to do us in also," said Yvgeney.

"That means that every one in that room was marked for death this week except maybe the reporters and that guy from Maine who was on vacation," said Wally. "What was so important about that fake desk that someone has to get killed for?"

"I think insisting on interviewing Smith and your success in finding him has brought unwelcome attention to a lucrative business in forged and faked masterpieces," said Yvgeney. "The interior of the boat shop suggested a sophisticated operation—maybe global by the accents of the people we met. We three represent an unacceptable liability to some rich and probably desperate men."

Ed Brown, gone, mused Wally, we had some times.

"Tell me more about this man," Yvgeney said. "There must be a connection between the people in the auction hall and the workshop hidden on a wilderness shore line. Something we do not know yet. Something that killed the auctioneer. Something that made Smith laugh before he died."

"Brown was a character. Never played by the rules. He was smart enough to get away with it most of the time. He told me he went to a town in Eastern Washington to sell the contents of an old hotel. No one greeted him when he got there, so he picked the lock and ran the auction that weekend. Sold all the furniture and fixtures. When he was leaving town on Monday, he drove by another hotel and recognized the name. It was the hotel that had hired him."

"He auctioned the wrong hotel?" Lucy asked, stroking Yvgeney's hand.

"Yup. He told me he beat the charges."

"He did not," said Yvgeney. "I have seen his file."

"You looked at his file? What file?" Wally said, incredulous.

"Interpol. Wally, I told you I work for the United Nations. I have seen your file also."

"I have a file?" Wally was thrilled. "What did it say?"

"It tells me you are a good citizen except for an indecent exposure incident when you were in college."

"That wasn't my fault." Wally said. "I was in the band. The tuba player smuggled a bottle of Jack into the football game in his horn. Got the wind section stink-o. Taking off our clothes seemed like a good idea at the time."

"Wally," Lucy giggled. "You dirty boy."

"Tell me more about the auctioneer," Yvgeney said.

"He hated to lose. Sometimes it made me nervous. There was one time on the road, at a flea market, when I beat him to a great Stickley chair and he never forgave me."

"For finding a chair?"

"It was a special chair. A Morris chair. An old-fashioned recliner. One of Stickley's best. It had a neat bend to the arms and small square spindles like Frank Lloyd Wright. Rare. It was worth five, maybe seven grand back then."

Neither Lucy nor Yvgeney interrupted.

"I found it out in the flea market line-up at dawn, still in the farmer's pickup, covered with a tarp. I borrowed money from Brown to buy it and the asshole thought he was a partner. I told him I just borrowed some money to buy a chair. When I sold it for five grand, a few days later in the Midwest, I paid him back. With interest."

"What did you give him?" Lucy asked. "An autographed picture of yourself?"

"No. There was this really great microbrew that was only for sale near Akron. I knew Brown would enjoy it. He loved beer."

"You gave him a case of beer for interest? How much did you make on the chair?" Lucy said.

"A six-pack, actually. The stuff was expensive."

"How much did you make?" Lucy asked.

"Four thousand, more or less."

"You made four thousand dollars on this fellow's money and you gave him a six-pack of beer?"

"He loaned me 500 dollars. I paid him back in two days and gave him a gift."

"And you wonder why he hasn't forgiven you?"

Wally gulped, realizing that Ed Brown had taken his forgiveness to the grave.

Evening was falling on an overcast Canadian summer day that promised rain. The roadside had changed from trees and pasture to a parade of cheap motels, stoplights, and strip malls.

"Ed never cared much about money, but he loved to spend it," Wally said. "Winning meant the hunt, the stalking, the haggling, not the pay-off. To him it was a game. A game he didn't like to lose." He turned the parking lights on with the wipers as a drizzle of rain began.

Yvgeney's attention strayed back to his own thoughts. He found the waistband of Lucy's jeans as his hand wandered down her bare back under her shirt.

She leaned forward a bit.

He stopped.

She lifted her head and kissed his chin.

He whispered, "I will not let anyone harm you."

The danger, he thought, lay in the unanswered connections. Other than the invited press and that accidental visitor from Maine, everyone connected with the auction was either dead or in this Suburban. Had he met his enemy yet? This person intent on silencing Wally, Lucy and him? Was it that German he had clubbed with the aluminum bat, Mr. White Coat? The man was certainly an adversary. No, Yvgeney thought. He seemed more of a henchman than the brains. That old guy in pajamas who interrupted him in the cannery? No, a craftsman, brought to Port Alberni for a specific reproduction. Was there some unseen Mr. Big hiding out in his private castle and ordering up those deaths? Yvgeney doubted it. The pursuit was intense, more like personal zeal. Yvgeney had met his oppressor, and perhaps even knew him; he was sure of it. Who else would qualify as an enemy? The people he had run into since Tacoma were either dead, or driving, or flirting in the back seat.

Yvgeney's fingers slipped under Lucy's waistband.

She arched her shoulders and neck.

He hesitated, withdrew his hand, and draped his arm around her as before.

"Good tactics, Russian man." Lucy was disappointed and delighted. The man would never make it as a *GQ* model, she thought, but his eyes told her everything would be fine. He would be sure of it. His confidence looked good on his craggy face. And that pesky ringlet of hair begged to be adjusted. She nuzzled the calloused hand by her cheek and smelled cod.

"*Spaciba.*"

As they passed the billboard advertising the Chemainus murals, Wally's obsessive mind workedg ... obsessively. He directed a question to the back seat for a vote. "Do you guys think we can get that bark-covered sideboard in this Suburban?"

"I absolutely disapprove of any contact with your van," Yvgeney said. "Leave it alone until this danger is resolved."

"Don't even think of it, Wally," Lucy said. "You've got half the dodgy buggers in British Columbia trying to do us in."

Wally bit his lip, choked back a rebuttal. The dark windows in an anonymous vehicle were saving them at the moment. But he obsessed some more, riding a bubble of incurable optimism, dying to put this dining room set together to bust Rudy's balls. He was keen to rewire that cool operating room lamp. So he pushed ahead. "How about this. It's dark. We'll just drive by my van in the Walmart parking lot and I can check out the load. Come on ... we'll just look like another Walmart shopper."

Yvgeney hated the idea. Ten years in the Russian military had taught him to stay out of minefields. Everything connected to that van spelled trouble, and they were almost out of immediate danger. He liked the surprising love interest he was discovering as he snuggled in the backseat, longing for the safety of a ferryboat ride to the United States.

"I have to get the stuff home sometime. There are some really important things in that van. I promise I won't stop. I'll just cruise past like I want to find a parking space. Next week, I'll send a buddy the key and he can drive it home. Let me see if everything's still there," Wally said.

"I don't see any harm in a drive-by." Lucy knew the signs of whining that preceded a Walter Winchester antiquing obsession. Best to get it over with and return to covering their backsides.

Yvgeney was also thinking about backsides. His right hand still rested on the small of Lucy's back, two fingers trying to behave, tucked knuckle-deep under her waistband.

"Do not stop this vehicle when you make your inspection pass. We cannot attract any attention to this Suburban."

"Deal." A mural of a gold mine on a two story storefront to the right of Highway 1-A south flashed by. Chemainus loomed against a gloomy, overcast sky. A roll of thunder followed a flash of lightning. No floodlights on the murals. Good, Wally thought. He secretly liked Chemainus better as just a town.

A traffic light on yellow, then red, was visible ahead on the dark four lane. Braking taillights glowed ahead. The Walmart lot opened up on the right as the Suburban passed the intersection. Six or seven RVs were parked for the night at Cheapskate KOA, Wally's name for big box store parking lots.

The blue van was still there, by itself near the street, smaller than other Rvs or campers, but not out of place. Pools of light from the over-bright street lamps flowed over the end of the lot. The RVs and Wally's van sat in semi-darkness, briefly illuminated by the lights of Victoria-bound cars. Wally turned right. Walmart was closed and only a few vehicles remained, save the campers and the van.

Yvgeney did not feel good about Wally's diversion. Wally didn't seem to heed the peril that swirled around them and how far they were from safety. The thought of Lucy and a warm bed crossed his mind, but he drove it away. He was tense.

They passed a dark Winnebago and a Ford F-250 with a camper, then Wally's van. Wally tried to drive like a tourist or a disappointed, tardy shopper. It was hard to see into the van as they made their slow pass in the poorly lighted lot. The traffic lights on 1-A changed and a slug of travelers stepped on the gas. Headlights flickered across the side door. Wally's heart sank. The passenger door was wide open.

"Damn it. Damn it. Someone's broken into my load," Wally hissed. He wheeled the Suburban around and circled his van again. He slowed down and nearly stopped. He cursed again when he saw his prized sideboard open to the world at 10:30 on a busy Canadian summer night.

Without warning, Wally shifted into park; the Suburban halted, shuddering. He jumped out, headed for his van.

"No!" Yvgeney shouted, but Wally was already gone. Yvgeney shook his head in disbelief. "That *idiot!*" he said to Lucy as he watched their anonymous retreat to Camano Island unravel.

She rolled her eyes skyward. She understood the madness. At Wally's level of collecting, lack of impulse control was looked upon as an asset.

Yvgeney reached past Lucy and opened the driver's window. He whispered loudly, "Get back now, you fool. You will get us all killed."

Wally heard nothing as he reached the van. The sideboard was visible in there, lying on its side. A gray, shiny arm from the surgical lamp was barely discernible. Thank God, he thought. Lock it up again. Hope for the best. And get the fuck out of here. I know that the Russian's pissed off now, and probably Lucy, too. But the door was open.

Another slug of traffic passed the lot, illuminating Wally and the van's interior. He saw a body. More headlights, this time from the Suburban, flashed twice. Yvgeney or Lucy signaling *get the bloody hell back here!*

Wally recognized the crumpled corpse and smelled the putrid odor of Don Smith rotting away between the front bucket seats. Another flash from Yvgeney's headlights told Wally the man's head had been bashed in and a woodworking tool, maybe a chisel, sprouted from Smith's chest.

"Christ."

"Get in here now!" Yvgeney was at the wheel of the Suburban. Despite his shock, Wally remembered to lock the van door when he closed it. He ran to the open Suburban passenger door and hopped in—and was greeted by angry stares. They drove as fast as they dared, south, into the night.

Yvgeney watched in the rearview mirror as they pulled out of the lot. A pair of headlights followed them onto the highway. "We have been compromised," he said.

Chapter Twenty

Route 1-A to Victoria, British Columbia

"You have the bone brain of a bird," Yvgeney shouted at Wally.

"He was there. Smith. Dead. I saw him. Right next to the sideboard."

"He was dead yesterday. I told you. I saw him at the park." Lucy teetered on the edge of fear and anger, but chose anger, as it was much less frightening.

"But he was in my van. Stunk like hell. I'll never get the smell out of that furniture."

"You'll never see that furniture. It'll end up in an impound lot on Vancouver Island and now the police are wanting you for an interview." Lucy said.

"I didn't kill him," Wally said.

"You know, I think we should have taken the antiques from the van back there." Wally was the passenger now. The traffic was thicker as the buildings of Victoria proper replaced the empty strip malls and billboards that marked the north end of town.

Lucy had a difficult time keeping her mouth shut. "You're determined to get us killed, aren't you? It's only a piece of wood and another bleeding lamp. Your house is filled with too many bloody lights already."

"But I think it was my screwdriver sticking out of Smith's chest. I always have a big-handled driver in the glove box. Maybe it was my chisel, come to think of it. I couldn't see the blade. Now the cops are going to think I did it and I'll never get my sideboard back. It'll be evidence."

Yvgeney's mind was on high alert. He watched the rearview mirror and paid attention to every vehicle they met or passed in the steady downpour.

He had not found the connection yet between the auction and the mayhem they were mixed in. It was obvious to him that whoever was behind this pursuit had moved Smith's body and stuck Wally squarely in the middle of a murder that could implicate them all.

"Maybe the judge will let you have your last meal off that serving table and maybe they will hang the chandelier in the chamber when they administer the lethal injection." Yvgeney thought Wally brightened a little at the thought.

"They have witnesses who can place you in Port Alberni, where he lived, and others who can place you and us in Chemainus after the assault."

"It'll be a great story for TV if I get that sideboard on the Antiques Road Show. They're coming back to Seattle, you know."

"Yeah, Wally. Who's going to take it there? Your next of kin?" Lucy said.

"Two people are dead and you do not know who is behind it, my friend. Your best situation would be to turn yourself in to the American police and let them sort it out." Yvgeney was looking for *Ferry* signs through the fast-moving wiper blades. He remembered evenings in Moscow. The last thing a car owner did at night was disconnect the wiper arms to keep them safe from theft till morning.

Two *Ferry* signposts came up at a corner—one pointing left and one pointing right.

"Where do we go, Wally?"

"There are two ferries off the south end, not counting the Anacortes run. That one only runs twice a day. It gets us back to where we entered. The other one shoots straight across the sound to Port Angeles, Washington."

Yvgeney stopped at the corner, mindful of the pursuers at their rear.

"It is almost 10:45," he said. "Do they run boats this late at night?"

"I dunno. They run double boats till fall. I know that Tsawwassen runs late. It's a commute to the mainland from there."

"Which one is closer?"

"The Black Ball to Port Angeles," Wally said. "It's right ahead at the other side of town."

A pair of larger headlamps began moving again when the Suburban leapt forward into the rain.

Lucy said, "There's another bloke that died last week. That friend of yours, Wally. The guy who ran off the cliff."

"Geoffrey, that's right!"

Yvgeney asked, "Did this fellow have any connection to the Tacoma auction house?"

"Don't know. Never saw him in the States. Gonna miss him. Boy, could he come up with good stuff. Us in the trade thought it was amazing that so many world-class rarities could be found on Vancouver Island."

Wally's head turned as he read the street name as they passed a signpost. "Turn right here, Yvgeney." Wally reached for the steering wheel. "Now," he said. "You're gonna miss it."

Yvgeney wheeled the Suburban onto a tree-lined lane of darkened parked cars and Edwardian townhouses with flickering TV light leaking from mullioned windows. He stopped. Windshield wipers batted against the hard, steady rain. The headlights of steady southbound traffic flashed across the rearview mirror like ducks in a shooting gallery. "All right, my friend, we are here. Why did you make us turn?"

"Geoffery's house is in a grove of trees just down the road. I want to give my condolences to the widow and give her my card in case she has any questions."

"Whore," Lucy said from the back seat. "Get us to the ferry, Yvgeney. Wally only wants to get first dibs on the woman's estate."

"The driveway's nearly in sight around the corner, for god's sake, Lucy. The woman must be heartbroken."

"What's her first name, Wally?"

He hesitated and said, "Alice."

"Liar."

Wally said, "Look behind us, Yvgeney. See any bad guys behind us? No. if anyone had followed us from the parking lot, they're not dogging us now. That quick right turn made us invisible again. You can thank me later. Give me five minutes."

Yvgeney said, "Can we get to the ferry on back streets if we continue on this road?"

"I've picked this city for 10 years. All these side streets up here lead to the west end of the harbor. I'm sure of it."

"I hate you both," Lucy said. "I vote for turning this thing around and getting on the bleeding boat."

Yvgeney said, "I must admit, Lucy, I favor the idea of back streets to the ferry. If we were followed, and I believe we were, they may be doubling back to try to locate us. I like the sanctuary of five minutes tucked into a dark driveway. Wally, will this big Suburban be hidden from the street if we go to this house?"

"Absolutely. It's tucked way back. Sits on a couple acres."

Yvgeney turned to Lucy's face in the dark behind him. "Tell me what you want to do. As the American cowboys say, *it's your call.*"

"It sounds like two to one in favor of a condolence visit," Wally said.

"Despite what your government tells you, Wally, the universe is not a democracy. Lucy did not ask for this trouble. She decides."

She said, "Go see your bloody widow, Wally. I'll be beside you. If her name isn't Alice, I'll scratch your eyes out."

"You better step on it, Yvgeney. We don't want to keep the poor woman up."

"There's the driveway," Wally said. "I told you it was up ahead. Turn here, after that big tree."

"I am having trouble with the English language," Yvgeney said as he entered a tree-lined drive. "Does the expression around the corner always mean 2.3 kilometers?"

"That's Wally-math, Yvgeney. Get used to it."

147

The Suburban rolled smoothly through leafy vegetation that, indeed, hid them from the street. Lights in the windows of a two story bungalow suggested the hour was not too late. Wally leaped out as the gear shift hit park, Lucy on his heels. Yvgeney closed his door more quietly and began a soggy circuit around the yard. Rain beat on his baseball cap and sent a cold trickle down his back. He zipped the front of his jacket higher to tighten the collar.

At the front door under a canopy, Wally pushed the doorbell and cleared his throat. A haggard woman's face appeared at the window. She opened the door to the chain.

Wally spoke to the crack of light. "Hey. Good evening. I'm Wally Winchester, friend of Geoffery's. Remember me? From the US. Camano Island. I've been here before. A couple of years ago. You served us tea and crumpets."

"I'm sorry. I don't remember you. Geoffery had many visitors over the years. Please forgive me. It's been a difficult week."

"I understand," Wally said. "I stopped to extend condolences."

"Do you know what time it is, sir?"

"We're on our way to the ferry to go off-island. It was my only chance. Say, do you know the time of the Blackball's last departure?"

"No." Behind the woman the phone rang. "I have a call," she said. "Thank you for your thoughts. Good night."

"Can I give you my card in case you need any assistance?"

She closed the door in his face.

Lucy pursed her lips. "Alice, huh?" she said.

A stiffening gust slanted the rain. Wally was looking at Lucy with a useless grin when the door opened again.

"Excuse me," the woman said. Lucy thought she looked three shades whiter than a moment before. "It was rude of me to turn you out into this weather. Would you like to come in and have a cup of tea?"

"Only for a minute," Wally said. "We have a boat to catch." He pinched Lucy's hip. She batted his hand away as she followed him inside.

Leaning into the pelting rain, Yvgeney moved through puddles of standing water near the maze of sheds and storage units in the back yard. A pair of muddy auto tracks, winding among the structures, disappeared into the trees. He saw no evidence of recent activity. He pulled his cap brim down and continued his circuit.

"Wally hasn't introduced us. My name is Lucy, and you?"

"Beth. Beth Buckingham."

Lucy watched tears filling the widow's eyes, took her hand and said, "I'm sorry for your loss."

"You're British."

"Born on the bank of the Thames, my mum told me."

"And you're young, you're just a child. You shouldn't be mixed up with this."

"Mixed up with what?"

"The Germans." She glanced out the windows at the evening storm. The teapot whistled. "Excuse me," she said, glancing toward the front door as if she'd heard something. She withdrew.

Wally dripped water onto a fine Oriental runner. Lucy grabbed his wet arm. "We have to get out of here. I think the woman's expecting someone she's afraid of."

"Just a minute, Lucy."

Wally spoke in a robot voice as his eyes danced around the home. "See that floor lamp over there? It's Roycroft hammered copper with a Steuben Aurene shade. That bastard never told me he had one."

"The bastard's dead, Wally. Something's really wrong with this scene. After she got that phone call, your friend, *Alice*, or was it Beth, did a one-eighty and invited us inside. Why?"

"Look at that chair, Lucy. See that inlay? What's old Geoffery doing with this great stuff in his living room?"

"Rotting away, I suspect. Pay attention, idiot."

"Look at all this green pottery. Wow, the sideboard of my dreams. He still has it."

"You've never been in this house before, have you? You told us you visited here often."

"I never got an invitation inside, actually. Geoffery kept me to the outbuildings. His wife brought us tea out there. In the back."

"You're sicker than I thought. I'm leaving. Now. I'm going to tell Yvgeney to leave directly and take me to the ferry. If you're with us, fine. If you remain here, I don't care."

"Here's our tea," the widow said, returning. She placed a silver tray with sugared confections and matte green cups on the massive oak sideboard that occupied most of the living room wall. Lucy looked at the front door, relented, and accepted a steaming cup. She noticed the woman's hand shaking as she poured the tea.

"I love this sideboard, Beth," Wally said. "I fell in love with it when Geoffery had it in the Fort Street shop a couple of years ago. I just didn't have the 20,000 dollars he was asking. It's the most impressive piece of Roycroft furniture I've ever seen. It's good that he decided to bring it home. He told me he sold it."

"He did sell it. This is another one."

Wally's eyes went wrong. His lip quivered. He leaned closer to examine the dark finish. The rich, brown patina seemed straight and right. Roycroft legends talked about vats of acid, mixed with the day's scrap iron, that gave the oak a hundred years of darkening in a dunk. Wally had handled his share of Roycroft items. The finish on this sideboard felt original.

He lifted a mottled green vase off the top and asked the widow if he could look under it for a pottery mark. The ashen woman shrugged. He looked for the Fulper mark and found it. A dark spot where the Fulper sat was darker. It contrasted with the rest of the broad plank top. Wally swiped the dark shadow to wipe away the dust around it, but the contrast remained.

He looked at the chiseled shop-mark, the *R* inside the orb and cross. He asked, "This piece of furniture is old, isn't it?"

"Of course," the widow said.

"Does the sun hit it during the summer?"

"Wally, we have to go," Lucy said. She watched the widow glance at the windows. She saw fear.

"We get sun on this wall all year," the woman said, distracted.

A framed snapshot sat on the dark surface that Wally now knew was recently colored with aniline dye. He picked it up. Ed Brown and a younger Geoffery, a European city at their back. "Geoffery and Ed Brown were friends?"

"They go to Europe three …" she stopped. "They used to go to Europe three times a year. Buying trips, he told me. Ed supplied Geoffery with many wonderful finds."

"Wally, we have to go."

"Yes, Child, go." The widow said. "They're coming."

Yvgeney reached the Suburban and saw lights on the road outside the wooded lot. He walked closer, jumping from shadow to shadow and saw a line of vehicles and a huddle of men. Headlights glinting off automatic weapons was unmistakable. He turned and ran.

They met at the vehicle. Yvgeney had started the engine. "Get in," he said. The headlamps were off. Windshield wipers on high slammed across the window.

"There's people coming for us," Wally said.

"They are already here. Hold on." Yvgeney gunned the motor and drove across the yard toward the line of storage sheds and the rutted passage into the trees.

The deep ruts held the wheels as Yvgeney guessed his way forward. A light flickering through evergreen branches was his goal. As the Suburban cleared the grove he approached a quiet residential street. Rain-swept light from a street lamp glowed on the opposite side. A wood and wire gate blocked their exit. Yvgeney plowed through it and drove, lightless, through a Tudor neighborhood until he reached the north-south highway. He switched on the headlights and turned south.

Wally spoke first. "The auctioneer and Geoffery were in it together. I saw a picture of them together in Europe," he said as downtown darkness swallowed them.

"And now they are both dead. Did you see anything that leads to a living, breathing killer? Any other photographs?" Yvegeney asked.

"The widow told me Brown and Geoffery went abroad three times a year. Brown was feeding him merchandise. Probably bogus. The very cool Roycroft sideboard in the house is a fake. Two years in

Canadian sun won't fade an original surface. These crooks are good, but they're using the wrong dye."

Yvgeney liked the sound of the word, *bogus*. He added it to his bank of American slang. "Problem is,' he said, "someone is intent on killing us. Someone we have met, I think, but there is no one left alive to suspect."

The Victoria harbor appeared between buildings off to the right as they rolled down Government Street in the rain. The Empress Hotel, huge and Victorian, a survivor of the Great Canadian Railway Hotels, loomed upward to the left. Government House, with its uncountable rim of ever-burning lights, stood out against the overcast night sky.

A short right turn followed the curve of the deep-water inlet, a natural harbor that many years earlier had brought prosperity to the settlement.

They passed the glass-bottomed tourist boat, dark late at night, and turned toward the water's edge, hoping the last boat hadn't left.

"We would like to leave tonight," Yvgeney said to the ticket taker in her booth. "Is there still time?"

The middle-aged attendant grimaced and said, "The ferry leaves in 15 minutes. That should give you time to get through customs. Thirty-five dollars—vehicle, driver. And how many passengers?"

"Two others," Yvgeney said. He pulled out 60 dollars in traveler's checks, US funds.

"Let me calculate—"

"Keep it," he said, and drove down to the waiting dock below them.

The woman was about to pocket her 22-dollar tip when another vehicle drove up. A handsome, European-looking driver asked, "Can we still make the same boat that the car in front of us is on?"

"Plenty of room this time of night."

"This enough?" The driver waved a 100-dollar bill, impatiently, pressing her to reach out and take it.

"With the currency exchange and one—"

The Ford Explorer driver accelerated and drove toward the hulking shape floating in the water straight ahead. The stocky blonde male passenger remained silent.

The customs man looked tired. "Where do you live?"

"Moscow," answered the driver.

"Camano Island, Washington, USA," said the two passengers.

The agent looked at his watch.

"Any Canadian citizens with you?"

"No," said Yvgeney said, realizing that there was nothing to indicate why they had a Canadian vehicle.

"Any firearms or dangerous materials leaving the country?"

"No, sir."

"OK. First lane on the left." He didn't ask about the rustic legs and tabletops inside. It didn't look like a national treasure and there was one more car to clear through before he punched out.

The big side door was opened to the shore ramp and Yvgeney drove the Suburban in.

Wally always got a kick out of the huge side-entry vessels and was glad he didn't have an 18-wheeler to negotiate into a narrow slot as they parked along the weathered metal hull on the inlet side.

Twenty coats of old white paint softened the rivets and portholes that dotted the interior of the wall. Bright fluorescents cast a sepulchral glow over the scattering of trucks, RVs, and tourist vehicles that made up the late night run.

The conversation was stuck on villains. Yvgeney was running the list for the third time. "The auctioneer Brown, his wife, Smith, that camper, media people, you and me. Now this fellow from Fort Street. Who have we left out, Wally? Did you speak with this dealer from Maine, that camper?"

"I did, but for just a minute. His story that he was camping was really stupid. I figured he was there to snoop around, maybe try to buy an expensive desk cheap. I never figured he was a serious bidder. He didn't bid, now that I think about it."

Yvgeney turned the engine off, left the keys in the ignition. "I am going to take a walk around to see if I can find our enemy," he said, looking sternly at Lucy. "Keep the doors locked. And do not leave the car. Got it?" The warning was aimed at Wally. "Neither one of you leaves the car. No snacks. No bathroom. Understand?"

Wally and Lucy nodded.

Lucy crossed her legs and looked around for an empty cup. No romance if you pee in a cup on your first date, she concluded. Wally didn't count. She searched the interior for a plastic cup, finding nothing. Sighing sadly, she settled down to get to know her bladder pain.

Wally stuck his head out the window and looked around. The vehicle deck was deserted, the parking crew now topside. All the parked vehicles appeared empty and unthreatening. The Ford Explorer that had been behind them at the customs booth had been directed to the other side, near the entry door, probably to help balance the ship load. Swinging doors revealed a well-worn staircase to the upper decks.

"I'm sorry I got you into this mess, Lucy. I just wanted to write a story."

"Well, we're still alive, and I wanted some adventure, sweetheart," Lucy said, biting back the part about his dumb move back at the Walmart lot. "We'll get home and we'll be fine. I'll have a nice tub and a Russian to bathe with, and you can get back to your very understanding girlfriend."

"What's the story about you and our investigator?" Wally asked. "You two were getting pretty tight back there."

"I think he's quite an interesting man."

"Were you getting some in the backseat, you rascal? I thought I heard some moaning back there."

"The only moaning you heard was about your idiotic behavior, you fanatic. "Actually, I find him rather charming. He could have had the farm back there and he acted like a gentleman, almost. You could take some lessons from the man."

Someone knocked on the window and they both turned. It was not Yvgeney.

Wally saw a ghost peer through the tinted window. He nearly shit his pants. "Holy shit! It's Ed." He leaned past the steering wheel to crank down the driver's window.

Yvgeney walked around the coffee shop on level two. Looking for potential threats, he evaluated each passenger in the lounge. What he saw were a few tired tourists and business people who looked like they would rather be home at 11:15 on a Monday night. The moon had risen. Ahead, a necklace of lights signaled the Port Angeles shoreline and the US. A thousand three-foot waves stretched before him on the vast expanse called the Straight of Juan de Fuca, each one reflecting the moonlight like a sea of broken glass.

Two tough-looking men hunched over a map by the window. They were drinking coffee and looked like long-haul truckers. An angry mother with two whining four-or-five-year-old kids was browbeating her crestfallen husband at their table. Yvgeney's guess: Dad did not ask for directions, again, and now look what time it is.

Three college girls giggled in one corner. A businessman in a rumpled suit sat alone. Yvgeney figured he was probably wondering which wrong turn in his life had placed him on a midnight ferry to another flea-bitten Northwest town. He wrote him off. A couple stood outside along the rail, holding hands. If anyone is clever enough to send a team of lovers to assassinate us, he thought, then I guess I have met my match.

A flash of white caught the corner of Yvgeney's eye. *White Coat?* Yvgeney looked left, saw no one. The door to the outside deck was ajar. He dashed to the opening. A gust of wind hit him as he stepped outside. Glancing left and right, he saw no one.

Yvgeney looked down at the frothy Pacific Ocean, lit by moonbeams. It was a mild night. The wind in his face promised a warm sunny morning, but far below him, the waves looked cold.

He walked the circumference of the ferry on the outside decks and found them empty. One more canvass and I will go back to Lucy, he thought. Five minutes to the US shore.

"You're supposed to be dead. Rae told me on the phone!"

Ed Brown's smile made Lucy shiver. She didn't know this fellow Wally seemed so grateful to encounter and certainly didn't like that grin. Too many years on the London streets had hardened her to that ticket-taker's smile.

"Actually, Wally, you're the one who's dead, you fucking idiot. You couldn't leave well enough alone, could you?"

"What do you mean?"

"You and your goddamn snooping. You've ruined years of work. Years and years of a perfect scam. First Smith shows up, after trying to peddle that shitty copy of the kneehole desk from Seattle to San Francisco, and then you appear and start asking questions up and down the fucking coast."

"You called me and invited me, Ed."

"I called you to gloat, asshole. I never expected you to show up. Figured a 50-dollar cover would keep you away. Then you decide you're going to write a goddamned magazine article. I could lose millions if you ever write that story. Millions. The people I work for are ruthless. But you're not going to write that story, dimwit, because you and your meddling friends are never going to get past Port Angeles. At least you get to be buried in a scenic spot. I wanted to tell you personally, before you die. By the way, that's an interesting set of furniture you've got back there." He nodded at the back of the Suburban. "I'm going to enjoy auctioning it in Tacoma. Too bad you won't see it go down. Whaddaya think I can get for it?"

"Fuck you," Wally looked around for Yvgeney, but the car deck was empty of other pedestrians. "I don't even know why you're mad. I heard they found you face down in a vat of acid. The police are looking for Laura."

"Laura's fine. She's waiting for me back at Port Alberni. We have to break down our whole operation now and pack it away till the heat you stirred up calms down. Do you know how many people have died because of you?"

"Not counting us?" Wally was still having trouble taking this man's—this man he thought of as his old friend—pronouncements seriously.

"Three so far, old friend, and you three will make six. Smith was easy to kill. He's been a loose cannon for years now, showing off his 'early furniture collection'. We made all those goddamn pieces as study works. And he has to go to a major San Francisco auction house with the kneehole desk. And it wasn't even right yet."

"The Townsend desk?" Wally asked. The string between Tacoma and Port Alberni was beginning to bead together in his brain.

"Yeah, the San Francisco auction embarrassed us and almost got our operation uncovered. The desk never made the 15,000 reserve and we got it back. Last month Smith showed up at the Portland Antique Show with the desk again. I was lucky to get wind of it before he went East. We had to run the sale just to get it off the market. I was actually hoping he would set it on fire—it would have put the rogue piece to rest and ended it. That fool. We should have killed him years ago but he was such a craftsman with the period pieces. Besides, murder was never in the game plan until you blundered in. The bogus auction worked, you know, and everyone would have put it behind them as a bungled forgery, but you wanted to write an article for Arts and Fucking Antiques Magazine and started asking questions."

Wally looked around. "Don't worry about your friend, the Russian. Claus is going to introduce him to the Pacific Ocean. Maybe he'll float back to Siberia." A thin giggle escaped the auctioneer. He seemed embarrassed by it.

"You killed another fellow with your questions, you know. That happy-go-lightly refinisher in Campbell River. Now he can be with his pal, Johnny Cash, again. He could connect you to Smith at the cannery, and to us, when the bodies appeared."

"You killed that nice man? How could he hurt you, way up there? He was a cool guy."

"He's cool now. I'd guess room temperature. We're closing all the loopholes, Shithead. The Mission dealer from Victoria was another bump in our road."

Wally remembered: an accident on a cliff-side road.

"You? *You're* the brains behind that cannery/clock shop?"

"Just the North American brains. How do you think I can spend six weeks at a time in Europe? That's why I'm here, you know."

Wally sat silently behind the wheel of the Suburban. Lucy was leaning tensely against the window.

Brown thrust his head into the driver's window. "I have made and sold objects that reside in 27 museums and who-knows-how-many private and corporate collections."

"No shit." Wally, who had been trying to get stuff he'd found into museums for years, was strangely impressed, despite the obvious trouble he was in.

"All of them were produced in Port Alberni, and that's what you just fucked up."

Wally's quiet brain told him Brown didn't seem to have a gun or any other weapon that could harm them. His conscious brain reeled with the certainty in Brown's voice as he told his tale. Wally's artist brain was still perked up with a surprising degree of respect. Twenty-seven museums.

"Ed, I'm astonished. I had no idea. I'm so impressed. Why didn't you tell me this years ago? I could have kept it quiet. I could

160

have helped, for Christ's sake. Why didn't you take me aside and let me in?"

"No one could know, bucko. I have some ... partners ... German outfit ... they found me on one of the early Europe junking trips. They watched me rip off that building about to be demolished in Brussels. Liked my style, I guess."

Wally remembered the story. Ed and Laura, waiting for their container to be loaded for shipment to the US, watched workmen boarding up a street full of buildings complete with art nouveau leaded windows, art deco designs in the doors. City blocks of history, targets for the wrecking ball. Ed found the nearest tavern, hired the two meanest-looking thugs in the bar, and together they dismantled half the architectural details in broad daylight and added them to their container four hours before it was lifted onto the freighter.

"My German partners made a rule. No one in my antique network could know the truth. I screwed up when I bragged to you. These boys are very smart and organized and very fucking mean. I've seen their work and now so have you."

Wally just stared.

"Besides, loser, you've got this friendship thing overrated. I've been pissed at you ever since you beat me to the Morris chair in St. Charles. *I* found that chair, you fucking obsessed bastard."

"I found it, Ed."

"You know, I finally bought that chair back. I got it off the same little squink you sold it to on the way to Brimfield. What was that little town? Akron?"

"Cincinnati."

"Let's just say he felt obligated to sell it to me, reasonable, on my next trip East. I've owned it now for years. Years after you ripped me off. I've never even cleaned it. The bird poop stains add a little character to the piece. Of course, I won't sit on it." Ed looked into the car at Lucy. "What's your name, young lady?"

"Lucy, you prick."

"Lucy, you're charming,"

"Bugger off, you bloody creep. You make my skin crawl."

Brown smiled brighter.

"Say, I have a question," added Wally, fiddling with the keys in the ignition. He knew that what he heard was serious, but the improbability of his old sidekick running an international ring of forgers and wanting Wally dead seemed too bizarre to be afraid of.

"You're standing here. No weapon. No backup. Middle of the ocean—"

"Puget Sound," Brown said.

"Whatever," Wally said. "How are you going to kill me, you backstabbing bastard? Talk me to death? Bore me with your fantasies?"

"You think I'm going to carry a weapon through a border crossing that caught a terrorist last year? We don't need weapons. You and she are expected in Port Angeles."

He said the words slowly, dragging out the syllables, apparently still impressed with his own voice.

"There are some very competent people with very big guns expecting you and your vehicle. I figure you have 10 minutes left to breathe. I'm very confident in my people waiting for you at the ferry dock. I'll be there to meet you, too. Trust me, you're history." He reached in as if to pinch Wally's cheek but retracted his arm from the Suburban window.

Original Finish

The outside deck circled the bridge and continued to the port side. Yvgeney knew ships, and he knew that his quarry was somewhere in the moonlit darkness 40 feet above the frigid Pacific.

The lights of the US shore were close. He could make out the details of a ferry dock with a sprawling, sleeping town behind, glowing moonlit snow on the mountains at its back. He was looking carefully for the blonde man from the boathouse. The same man he slugged in Chemainus. The odds are good that he is here, he thought.

A deep, low-frequency shudder signaled the docking maneuver had begun. A lifeboat hung above him. He looked up, lifted the canvas, and peered inside. Empty, save the life jackets and medical kits fastened underneath the seats.

The blonde man touched an egg-sized knot behind his ear. He stood in a bend in the wall away from the windows to the lounge, smiling at the irony of the wooden bat in his hand.

The blow was terrific. Yvgeney felt the impact but not the pain. Visions of old framed paintings on the walls of his boyhood Moscow home flickered into darkness as he plummeted toward the water far below. The world went dark until the shock of cold water brought him back. In his first attempt to breathe, he inhaled frigid salt water. He forced it back out and thought, lungs burning, you're under the water. Find the surface. Military training kicked in. He turned his head sluggishly and saw a glow. He swam to it, breaking the surface with a gasp.

Inhaling deeply, trying to ignore a fierce headache, he felt the throb of massive propellers and kicked his legs instinctively to move away from the blades. Around him as he swam, he saw the shore lights eclipsed by the hull of the rumbling ferry. His vision blurred. He wiped his eyes, tasted blood when it reached his mouth. He swam toward the light, fighting the sweet embrace of unconsciousness.

Ed continued boasting. Winchester had been one of the only people he knew on the West Coast who could appreciate the magnitude of his secret, 10-year enterprise. Metal groaned as a bulkhead door opened. The German stepped onto the car deck. Empty-handed, his smile was sardonic. Spotting the auctioneer, he lifted a thumb.

"Your Russian friend is history, Winchester. I never should have invited him into the auction. His snooping and yours have cost us a great deal."

"No! No! You bastards!" yelled Lucy, whose fantasy had been growing in her heart. Shattered with the knowledge of that smile. "You fucker!" Tears poured from her eyes. She looked for anything in the front seat to attack these two with. Just to strike back. "Yvgeney," she said, and sobbed.

"I just wanted you to know." Brown and the blonde German turned away toward the Ford Explorer parked nearly out of sight behind a refrigerated 18-wheeler. Travelers began to trickle back down the stairs to their vehicles. The boat shuddered as the stern bumped the dock. Brown stopped and turned around. He shouted across the hollow ferry hull. "Remember that Harvey Ellis secretary with the inlay that sold up in Maine last year for 65 grand? I made that, and they never knew. It's at the Brooklyn Museum as we speak."

Brown and the German turned and walked away across the unreal blue-green glow of the vehicle deck.

164

Chapter Twenty-One

Black Ball Ferry Approaching Port Angeles, Washington

Vehicles on the lower deck started their engines. Lucy vomited on the floor. Her body was racked with fury and deep, bone-chilling fear.

"Don't leave yet, he's coming down soon," she pleaded, tears in her eyes.

"We gotta go, Lucy. He's gone. I saw it in the blonde fucker's eyes."

"No. He's all right."

"We have to pay attention. Stop. Listen. Someone is going to try to kill us when we disembark. Lucy, help me think!"

Wally started the Suburban and drove over to the exiting row of cars, feeling like a steer in the slaughterhouse chute. He watched as Brown's Ford Explorer cut off another car to get out of the boat before them. Gotta be first, as always, Ed, Wally thought, figuring the auctioneer was off to join his henchmen at the shore.

A hundred scenarios flashed across his mind. Movement off the boat from the vehicle deck stopped as an 18-wheeler jammed momentarily at the exit turn. He heard the transmission crunch and the air brakes hiss as the semi backed up, trying for a better angle.

Jump the customs line? He thought wildly. No. It's the Suburban they're looking for. Whoever was waiting to pounce would still have them in their sights.

"Lucy!" Her head was lolling around, eyes still wet. "We need a diversion. Think of something!"

Her face was grim. Without a word, she vaulted to the back seat and her clothing purchases, stuffed in a cloth sack.

Another truck rumbled loudly. Wally looked out the window. Forty feet of old timber on a log truck sat beside them. The driver gunned the big engine impatiently. A muscled, tattooed arm hung out the window on the Kenworth's passenger side. Wally leaped out and looked behind his vehicle. His hand reached deep into a side pocket where he kept his picking cash.

"Hey, you!" Wally said.

A large head wearing a grimy welder's cap looked down from the truck cab. A gruff voice said, "Yeah?"

"Want to make a thousand dollars?" The wad looked thick in Wally's fingers as he held the money skyward. It was a California roll with the big bills on the outside, but it got attention fast.

"I'm listening."

"We're in trouble and I've got to find someone to drive my rig through customs. Some people who want to hurt me are waiting on the dock. They know my vehicle, but they have no beef with you. A thousand dollars, cash." He wagged the bills in front of the man's face.

"You're some fucking smuggler and you want me to be in the hot seat, right?" His eyes followed the moving cash.

"These people want to hurt me and her." Wally pulled Lucy by the hand to the driver's side window. She looked wan but stylish in a colorful skirt and Day-Glo blouse.

"There's stuff in the back, but it's just some cabin furniture." Wally heard the roar of the jackknifed 18-wheeler as it cleared the exit. The line was about to move.

"If you want it, here's the money. Just understand that there's some bad-asses on the other side." He winced at the thought of placing the Stickley set in a stranger's hands.

"I'm not worried about nobody in this town," the man said, asking a question to the driver beside him. The door opened and a six-and-a-half-footer with red suspenders surrounding a massive gut climbed down. "Where d'ya want me to leave the vehicle?" he asked.

Wally smiled. "Do you know where the police station is?"

A short line of walk-off travelers stood ahead at the customs inspection queues. Suitcases were opened and IDs checked. Wally looked beyond the kiosk into darkness on the shoreline. Exiting traffic illuminated Brown's Explorer and another vehicle at the end of the dock. He looked behind him into the boat and saw the Suburban, windows up as he'd requested, four vehicles back in the car inspection line. Come on. Hurry it up, Wally thought, as he watched inspectors shine flashlights into a pickup truck bed. You have to leave first and draw the bad guys away from the dock. He looked to Lucy, caught her eye, and nodded toward their vehicle. She nodded back.

Barelegged, she walked up to the customs inspector's stand. As she passed the arch of the metal detector, no bells sounded. Wally held back and allowed some college kids with backpacks to get into the line ahead of him. He watched Lucy's magical smile as she presented her driver's license. He thought it was a remarkable performance, considering what her state of mind must have been.

As the college kids stood impatiently behind her, Lucy fussed with her backpack. She seemed to be having a difficult time with the bag, as it lay open on the polished concrete floor. Nice to be so limber, thought Wally, holding his ID in his hand.

Lucy cursed and unpacked her shirts again.

Wally saw commotion on shore as the Suburban pulled out and headed down the ramp. Dark windows reflected the dockside lights. Standing outside the customs line, he watched two vehicles turn and follow the big man driving Wally's borrowed rig.

Lucy straightened up as she saw Wally disappear into the dockside night. She snapped the backpack catch with one quick motion and bounded after him onto the pier.

Chapter Twenty-Two

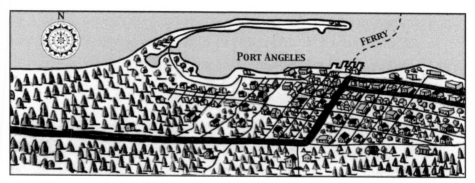

Port Angeles, Washington

The Port Angeles police parking lot was a few blocks from the Blackball Ferry terminal. At 10 past midnight, Wally and Lucy looked like two hikers with backpacks on a late night walk. The streets of Port Angeles were empty as they huddled against the chilly wind.

"I want to take a walk around the block once we spot the Suburban. I'm sure they have someone watching the lot, so don't pay any attention when we stroll by."

Behind a parked car, Lucy had slipped back into her jeans. Her Day-Glo blouse was tucked in like a T-shirt under a dark jacket and her hair was covered with a kerchief. Good Northwest camouflage. Wally took her hand as they strolled the sidewalk like lovers.

The parking lot behind the police station was at the opposite corner to the left, across the empty street. A pickup truck on high tires roared around a stop sign. Northwest amusement on a Monday evening. The throaty roar diminished as it throttled out of sight.

Wally saw that the Suburban was parked deep within the well-lit parking area. He was instantly relieved, smiling at the placement. It sat in the middle of six black-and-whites as if it belonged there. He saw an SUV and Brown's Explorer parked across from the lot on the side road.

"Look away, Lucy. Head down. Keep going past the corner. Then we take a right."

Wally and Lucy disappeared onto First Street West. Wally leaned against a wall and sighed. "Got any change?" he asked.

"Of course, sweetheart." It was a brave attempt at "everything's fine," spoken with a high English flourish. Shortly after midnight in a cold wind with scary people lurking about and a big, big hole in her heart that she wouldn't allow herself to look at yet, Lucy was having a hard time holding on to the illusion of calm.

Retreating behind the police station, Wally looked for a phone. They passed the big windows of the downtown stores of an earlier, more prosperous age, now offering consignment baby clothes and paint ball academies. Wally spied a pay phone on the corner.

"Good," he said softly. "One more thing to make sure of. Wait here, Lucy. Don't pick up any loggers."

She gave him a distracted-looking thumbs-up.

Jogging the block to the police station, Wally peered around the corner and spied his pursuers, still waiting. He didn't care. He looked to the parking area gate. It was open. Here you go, you fucker, he thought. Say hello to Homeland Security. He composed his spiel as he hurried back to the phone.

Lucy bent her head down as a pair of pickup trucks, side by side, cruised past her. Booming oversized base woofers rumbled in her ears. She lifted her finger toward the trucks as a string of catcalls spilled from the boys inside.

She jumped at the sudden sound of footsteps behind. She turned quickly to see Wally, slightly out of breath. "I think our friends are going to get a little visit," he said as he reached for the phone and dialed *9-1-1*.

After listening he said, "Hello, police? Thank God you're there—my name? Gustav Stickley ... S-T-I-C-K-L-E-Y... hey, I'm calling 'cause I just got off the Blackball Ferry. I saw two groups of Middle Eastern fellas, you know, them Arabs. They was acting suspicious-like, so I watched when they drove off the boat. Watched them park their cars next to the police station, right next to it, by the parking area ... yes, the Port Angeles police station. Don't know what they was up to but they hugged each other before they got into their cars ....What was they driving? Let me think. One was a white Ford Explorer, and the other one was a big, dark-colored SUV. I think it was a Lincoln .... You're welcome. God bless America."

He hung up.

A wobbly, overweight couple walked toward them up First Street. Intoxicated in some fashion, they passed Lucy and Wally without a look. Mumbling broken sentences punctuated by curses, they headed up the hill, continuing their slurred debate. A police car, lights flashing, came zooming in from the east and turned down the street next to the station.

Another car angled in from the opposite direction on the one-way street, lights revolving, sweeping spotlights on the surrounding building walls.

Wally ran to the parking lot and reached the Suburban. Lucy was close behind. Through the chain-link fence he saw the confrontation. Six large men stood defiantly arguing with a contingent of Port Angeles Blue whose weapons were drawn. One of the large men spotted Lucy and Wally; he bolted into the street, alerting his friends, only to be tackled by two officers. A scuffle broke out. Another police car arrived and emptied as the thugs were forced to the ground and handcuffed. One of them pointed at Wally across the road and screamed. Wally aimed a middle finger toward the melee, opened the Suburban door and retrieved the keys from under the seat. He hopped in and turned the ignition. The Suburban started up. He uttered silent thanks as he slammed the car into gear and drove through the open gate to freedom. The flashing faded in the rearview mirror as he zigzagged up the streets leading to the hills behind town. On the fourth corner up from First Street, he turned the headlights on.

"Where'd you get the idea of Middle Eastern terrorists?" Lucy asked as they drove through a quiet neighborhood.

"Beats me. It seemed to be the right thing to say at the time."

"It was brilliant," she said, squeezing his hand. She held her other thoughts at bay.

Exhilaration pumped them both. Twelve-thirty in the morning seemed oddly fine but they were running out of road and energy as the grade grew steeper.

"We can't go east toward Sequim or west out to the peninsula in this rig, you know, Lucy."

"Yeah, I'm sure you're right, sweetheart. Got any ideas?" The illusion of safety was boosted by the gutsy escape.

"I know a person who lives up in the hills to the west. We need some sleep. She'll let us stay there for sure. Marla and I go way back. We can stash the car and catch our breath."

Lucy was not looking forward to quiet time. The loss of Yvgeney filled her head but she'd held the sadness back during the escape. When she caught her breath she could let out the pain.

The stout Suburban had no trouble with the twisting mountain road to Marla's Lodge. Blackness to the right suggested drop-offs of unknown depths as the switchbacks zigzagged up the invisible foothills.

The moon was low to the left, but it still illuminated the cleft of a pass and the flatter meadows beyond. Trees were shorter here. Second-growth babies, 60 to 80 feet. A huge stump of a giant Douglas fir sat low and dew covered the field. A pointing road sign said:

MARLA'S LODGE

Rafting, Outfitting, Yoga
X-Country, You Name It.
By Appointment Only 555-2759

NO AROMATHERAPY

The driveway crossed a meadow and entered a forest backed by the looming pyramids of the Olympic Mountains. Weariness was closing Wally's reaction times to short moments of alertness. He cursed as the rutted road bounced the furniture around in the back of the Suburban. The forest parted to reveal a moonlit clearing with a steep-walled cliff beyond. They drove down the uneven cow path leading to three log structures and a parking area at the edge of a roaring white-water stream. Wally nestled the Suburban between two four-wheel drive rigs and gratefully shut the engine down.

After 20 seconds of knocking a hammered copper kayak paddle against a massive quarter-sawn oak door, it opened an inch and a woman's voice said, "I've got a gun aimed at your heart. What do you want at this hour?"

"Marla, it's me Wally. Wally Winchester. Open the door, I'm in trouble."

It opened. Wally admired the Craftsman-style lanterns hung from sconces inside and stared into the face of the woman he'd just awakened.

Marla wiped sleep from her eyes as she faced them in the foyer. She was short and wore a fuzzy robe like a chief's blanket as she stood there.

Wally's heart bumped as he looked at his old friend. Tiny wrinkles across a darkly suntanned face suggested 10,000 days outside. Her unkempt pillow-hair sprang sideways, but she was alert and focused.

"We need to crash, Marla." Wally spoke through a haze of exhaustion.

"I'm Lucy."

"Marla."

"Hi."

"We're in a lot of trouble." Wally said. "There are some terrible people who want to hurt us. I don't think they'll find us here, but this could put you in some danger."

Lucy said, "Send us off if you don't want to be involved, please. I would if I were you."

"Get in here and close the door," Marla said.

Wally said to Marla, "Do you have something to cover the Suburban with? That's the vehicle they're looking for."

"I've got some tarps in the boathouse. I'll take care of it. Go get warm by the fire."

Original Finish

When Marla got back, Wally and Lucy were lying on the blue Kazak rug, sound asleep under a light fixture hanging from a 20-foot iron chain. Wally had sold her the fixture 15 years before.

Pulling a blanket over Wally's shoulders, Marla returned to bed.

A couple of hours later, Lucy still cried.

Chapter Twenty-Three

Elwa Canyon, above Port Angeles, Washington

"Wake up, Wally. You've got trouble."

Wally's dream of a Frank Lloyd Wright yard sale popped and dissolved into Marla's determined face.

Lucy, eyes swollen and bloodshot, stood on wobbly legs to button her jeans.

"I went down to the road to check for mail." Marla told him. "I saw them coming from the top of the pass. Four vehicles, moving fast. I figure we've got two or three minutes to get on the water."

"We?"

"The water's high this time of year. The river's the only way out. I'll have to take you."

"The water?"

"Come on. Grab your things." Wally winced; his bladder was about to burst.

"You can pee off the raft." Marla had, no doubt, seen that pained look before.

They ran on rubber legs down to the river. Two inflated six-man rafts sat beached and tethered on the rocky shoreline. The river was a couple of dozen feet across, a fast-moving blanket that rippled over a rocky bottom.

"Get your vests on, *buck-o-roos.*" Marla positioned Lucy in the stern and gave her a paddle. Wally, she placed in the bow. As she climbed aboard, taking the middle bench and its pair of oars, she said, "The runoff from the spring melt bumps the Elwa up to a Class 3 series of ripples over six-foot boulders. You kids are in for a wild ride."

The sound of a closing car door reached them over the hiss of the river. "Off we go," Marla, said as she pushed the inflatable into the current with her oar.

Wally heard a series of soft reports, like gunfire, echo off the steep incline to the left as the current caught the craft broadside and sent it spinning down into the rapids.

"Sounds like they're shooting." Marla hunched over as she grabbed for the oars in the middle. "Best keep your head down till we drop over the percolator." All three flattened as the cabin disappeared behind a jumbled granite outcrop. The current quickened and the roaring sound grew louder.

"The percolator?"

"Funny little rapid ahead, feels like rafting through boiling water. It's OK. Don't worry. It's fun. This was all still water till they blew Dam One."

The canyon deepened, frothing cauldrons loomed ahead. With Marla pulling left and right on the paddles, shouting "Paddle now!" to Lucy in the stern, the raft rode the washboard waves. Wally cheered as the raft squirted through the narrow cleft into a calmer, wider flow. They were wet, and Marla grinned.

The calm disappeared as the canyon narrowed and the bottom fell out of the pool. The water quickened in the chute of river rolling down a deep ravine. Marla laughed and pulled the craft firmly to the softer passes through the foam. A dark stain grew steadily higher on the cliff sidewalls. Greenery clung to niches in the rock.

"That's the old high-water level that built up behind Dam One," Marla said as she pulled hard on the left oar to keep them in a safer channel. "All these runs are new to paddlers, at least for the last 80 years. The salmon and the river people got their water back. Ain't it grand?"

Five hundred feet of limestone, 100 million years of seabed sediment, bent and twisted by the North Pacific plate, rose nearly vertically. Broad bands of dark stone topped the walls above them.

They sat motionless in a quiet pool, a respite from the relentless drop, where the cliffs opened and formed a bowl. The water stain on the canyon walls continued uninterrupted. A band of green vegetation filled the hillside above.

"It'll take years for the flora to grow back down to the new shoreline, but it'll happen." Marla said as she caught her breath. "This is my favorite place along the upper section. You can see nature winning here as each new start takes hold. This is where I usually leave the older guests. It's a two-mile hike back to the lodge."

"You can reach your road from here?" asked Lucy. "I can climb back up and get the Suburban?"

"It's a scramble up the bank, always, but sure you can." Marla said. If you avoid the bad guys at the lodge, you can pick us up at the old dam site downriver. It's five miles farther down the road for a car. There's a takeout there, and a parking area."

"We need to escape these men, Wally," Lucy said. "I want to get the Suburban and we can be off. I'll meet you down below. Your friend doesn't need our trouble."

Wally looked up at a treacherous slope, ending in green vegetation high above the river. "You're not a mountain climber," he said.

"Wally, I'm going. You're not in charge of me. We have to get back safely or Yvgeney's death will go unreported. He must have family. The police can help us if we get back to Camano." Her mouth trembled.

Wally reached into his sock, extracted the Suburban key, and handed it to Lucy. "Be careful," he said.

Lucy climbed out onto the gently sloping shore and pushed the boat back into the current. "You, too." She stifled a sob as she began the climb.

The raft picked up speed, and Marla started to pull on her oars.

"The canyon gets nasty up ahead. Better get ready for some fun. We takeout about a mile downstream at the last good shoreline. The river's not safe past the dam."

Wally spotted the other raft. It appeared around the canyon bend, an inch-long yellow speck about a quarter-mile behind.

"Fuck."

Marla shrugged, surprisingly calm, and said, "The next section is the nasty part, Class 5 with undercuts down to the dam site. Your friends are going to learn to swim real soon. Better check the straps on our vests. We could be in the water, too."

The river quickened and the drop steepened as the canyon rose again to squeeze them between its walls. The roaring got louder. The choppy surface was chaotic, granting no easy passage down the building waterfall. The raft flipped vertically as it slapped a standing wave. Marla sat suspended for a second, feet dug in and paddles flying. She fell backward as the raft flopped down the foamy chute.

She bellowed, "Yahoo!" with seeming pleasure while Wally held on tight and tried to retrieve his breath.

The river rushed up suddenly to pin them under an overhanging wall. Marla cursed and pushed against black granite with her oar, sending them back into the tumult. Wally had the sensation of falling as the river dropped. The raft was airborne for a moment before smacking the water again.

"Hey, we got some air," Marla squealed. Wally choked as he caught his breath. He looked back at the canyon cut, watching for the danger that followed them somewhere close behind.

The river calmed a little as the canyon walls opened to a gentler slope. Looking backward to the crack that had just ejected them, Wally looked up into the waterfall of boiling white he'd just survived. A flash of yellow disappeared behind a wave and came into view again at the top of the falls. It looked like four people in the raft. It vanished and repeated its appearance.

"Shit. They're still with us."

"They must be locals if they got through that," Marla said. "No bother. We won't have to worry about them after the Margarita Shaker. With the water this high, there's only one safe passage through that mess and nobody knows it but me. Buckle up."

"Margarita Shaker?" Wally asked.

"Just hang on tight and listen to me."

The roar turned into a freight train sound as the raft fell over the wall. Thirty feet of freefall plunged the raft 10 feet into churning white chaos. Marla pulled the prow up with a mighty surge of her paddles and the raft popped up like a bobber into the choppy foam.

"I love that," she exclaimed, baring her teeth in an exultant grin. Wally tried but failed to get his voice back as he grasped for air and balance. He watched the cliff sides rise to an unimagined height as he lay back and exhaled.

"We have to takeout up ahead," Marla said. "This is the top of Dam One. There's a road handy. Anyway, the river below can't be run. We can meet your friend here when the coast is clear."

The Margarita Shaker. Wally concluded it was well-named.

Lucy's footing crumbled at the same time her outstretched hand found a solid grip on a rocky ledge. She didn't risk a look at the drop-off beneath her. Morning sunshine lit the cliff tops across the river gorge. Shivering, wet and cold, frightened and grieving, she climbed on. She looked longingly across the canyon, bathed in the promise of a perfect day. A cold breeze raised goose bumps and did nothing to lessen the numbness of her fingers.

She sat and rested on a flat, safe shelf, feet dangling over the roaring stream far below. The path appeared nearly vertical ahead. She wanted to cry again. Another cold breeze trickled down from the trees and bushes above. Starting her climb again, she chose a rock-filled gap that split the cliff face and started up again. Aware of the 40-foot drop-off behind her, she reminded herself to test each grip and foothold.

Lucy had no mountain training, preferring the first floor bistros and Amsterdam hash bars to cliffs and ropes and pitons, but fright and adrenaline and growing anger pushed her forward.

The tree root handhold was welcome. Above it, she saw the eastern sky. She clambered up the root onto a grassy slope and lay back gasping, feeling sunlight warming her frigid limbs.

Mindful of the people following them, Lucy kept to the shadows of a copse of young maple trees till she spotted the crushed-stone road they had driven late the evening before. Reaching it in a few long strides, she stood alone under the blue dome of sky.

When she heard the rumbling of distant motors farther up the road, she found a grove of prickly briars at the roadside and hunkered down like a rabbit in a thicket. A line of shiny four-wheel-drive vehicles rushed past, down into the valley. Road dust and exhaust behind them glowed yellow, backlit by the rising sun.

When silence returned, she emerged and headed up the gravel drive, thinking how much she missed Yvgeney. She thought about the confidence and resolve behind that darling little cowlick curl. Lucy had known her share of suitors but few of them, in the long run, had sufficient good character. She felt the memory of a callused hand on her back. She thought about the strength in his face as he plowed through the Port Alberni fog at full throttle. She remembered the first time she saw him, holding a baseball bat aloft after he saved her life. Another tear fell as she entered the grove of trees by the lodge.

The Suburban appeared to be unmolested. A dust-covered Subaru beside it was empty. Staying to the cover of the forest, she circled the house to the riverbank, saw that the other raft was gone. Keep your head down, Wally, she thought, realizing her friend had pursuers behind him on the river. Back at the Suburban, she cupped her eyes and peered through the darkened windows, seeing no boogiemen in the back seat. Wally's load of furniture was still safe inside. Silly man, she thought. Silly, obsessed, and in danger. She adjusted the bench seat forward and started the Suburban.

There was a problem with takeout above the upper dam. Marla explained the importance of making it to shore before they reached the gap in the canyon ahead. Broken pinnacles of concrete and rebar rose from the river and framed a drop-off of undetermined height. The river flattened before it cascaded over the breach that opened the waterway to the Pacific Ocean far below. As they floated toward the tall dam remnants that once held back spring flooding, they saw the greeting party parked above them in the takeout area.

"That's no good." Marla said.

"I guess that's our welcoming committee."

"They're blocking our exit, damn it. We need to get off the river here." Marla strained with her oars to eddy out and halt the raft's progress before they floated into the pool above the dam and shooting range.

"Can we exit on the west side?" Wally shouted over the deafening roar. He looked to the right and saw sheer, vertical walls.

"Too steep."

Marla launched forward off her seat and crumpled face down at Wally's feet, followed by the loud report of a high-powered rifle. The gunfire echoed repeatedly as it bounced back and forth between the walls. "I'm hit," she said.

Behind him, Wally saw the pursuing raft approaching rapidly, silhouetted against the sun-drenched western wall. He saw only two figures in the boat.

Instinctively, he pushed the raft back into the river flow with a paddle to the cliff face. The current pulled it back downstream, toward the hired guns waiting at the river's edge. Marla moaned and tried to get up but failed. Wally grabbed the oars as he took her seat in the center. He stared at a spreading crimson stain flowing under her shirt, red streaks on the white cotton. Fresh blood oozed from a tear in the fabric above her shoulder blade. Ahead, he saw commotion on the shore.

More shots rang out as he rowed, head down, toward the still water above the breach.

I heard it. Jesus Christ, I heard it. Holy shit! The unmistakable sound of a spinning bullet faded instantly as a high-powered round spiraled past Wally's ear.

"Don't go through the dam break," Marla ordered, face still pressed against the floor. "It can't be run. It's all unknown in there ... with a waterfall."

"We have no choice."

As he felt the unrelenting pull of the vortex beyond and below the gaping hole that was once a dam, Wally lifted his head. He saw four people with rifles scrambling down the bank toward the water's edge, pausing to aim and fire as they descended. He was surprised when the rafters behind him gave up the pursuit and rowed furiously, pulling for the shore. Thank God for small favors, he thought.

Wally felt the water fall away as the raft sailed through the jagged concrete breach. He screamed in fright as he and Marla plummeted into a cold dark chasm of frothy waves.

Marla struggled to get up, finally flopping her back against the forward seat. The front of her shoulder was brilliant crimson.

Wally felt the raft stabilize as it rode a surging tongue of water downward. It gave him a moment to think and look around. He caught a glimpse of the horizon through the gaps in the trees below. Distant shoreline smoke stacks and a cloudbank covered Vancouver Island across the water.

He did his best to row, but the raft flipped up without warning, nearly tipping Marla into him.

"Stay to the right if you can," shouted Marla. "I think there's a way through this gap, but I've never tested it. Too dangerous, even for me."

Wally found his voice and said, "Well, today you get your chance." The rock wall caught the rounded corner of the raft, sending it spinning back into a surging trough.

"Paddle right. Paddle right! You've got to get control before the next drop." Marla tried to sit up but couldn't catch her balance in the chaotic tumbling down the flume. "Pull, you stupid bastard," Marla yelled.

"I'm trying!"

The oars pulled at the river, and the dizzy spiral slowed.

"There's a big rock ahead around the bend. We're lucky the water's high. Maybe we'll catch enough flow to cover the boulders in the slot. Wally, listen to me, for once. When you see the split in the river you have to get the raft to the left side. The right channel is undercut and steep. That's where Billy died." She paused. "On the left side at least there's a chance. No one's tried it since."

The river flowed downward with terrifying speed. A narrow hundred-foot cut in the mountain slapped the raft against the wall, where it rolled upward and the fearsome water pressure began to fill the nearly vertical craft.

"Pull, pull with your right paddle."

Water swirled around Wally's lower knee, pinning the raft against the cliff and slowly pulling it under. Screaming with pain, Marla grabbed the paddle off the floor and jammed it upward against the stone above.

The raft bobbed to the surface and instantly hit another wave as the river carried them around the bend.

"Now get us to the left. Hurry." Marla was back on the floor. Tears mixed with foamy water on her sopping face.

He pulled with both hands and felt the boat respond. Over his left shoulder a thrust of pitch-black stone split the rapids ahead. He pulled again and again, feeling progress against the inexorable gravity of the drop.

"Pull more."

They were heading directly toward the towering boulder. Wally rowed fiercely but the river current held the raft. He strained on the oars again and felt the raft thump against the rock mass. The raft swung clockwise as it slid back into the current. Wally flailed again and caught some water, pulling the craft slowly into the left side flow.

The fast current caught them again, whiplashing them into the slot in the wall ahead. Water dropped in 10-foot surging stair steps and the raft plummeted down the narrow chute into hell.

The last thing Wally saw, as the tumbling began, was a yellow raft disappearing behind the boulder to the right.

The damaged raft twisted sideways, filled with water, and emptied as the wave tipped them over into the freezing waterfall. The cold instantly took Wally's breath away but he grabbed the trailing rope and pulled his head above the water. The frightful drop continued steeply downward as he struggled to catch his breath. Carried down the mountain in a white corridor of crashing waves, he felt the roundness of giant submerged boulders as the bottom rolled by under his feet. A yank reminded Wally that he was still connected to the raft. Risking a sideways glance, he spied an arm draped over the rounded side and saw the determined grimace on Marla's glistening face.

Another wave covered his head. When he popped up seconds later, Marla was gone. The empty raft surrendered again to gravity and rushing water and pulled him over the edge into a freefall to an unknown level below.

A huge hand of water held him under as the descent abruptly ended. Wally tried to struggle against the pressure, but the force was too awesome for a human's strength. The rope around his wrist tightened and yanked him upward as the raft popped onto the surface, dragging him back to air. He grabbed a cold wet breath and the raft bobbed down the river, pulling him behind.

The river flattened, moving swiftly through the notch. Trees appeared closer to the waterline. Ahead, the cliff melted into forested shoreline as the river flow bent again. Alone, Wally pulled himself up and flopped forward over the side into the gently bouncing raft.

"You can have my Stickley chandelier back if I don't make it."

Wally spun around and saw his friend's wet hair as she peered over the side again, her good arm draped over the rounded edge.

"NOT," she said in a painful attempt at a smile. "You're never getting that fucking fixture back."

A horn blared from the shore. Looking up, Wally saw Lucy standing beside the Suburban. She was waving her arms and shouting something lost to the din of the river.

They kicked and hand-paddled close enough to the bank for Lucy to jump in waist-deep and pull them to the shore.

"Boy, that's cold," she exclaimed. "I saw a bunch of cars up beyond at the dam. They were busy at the river, probably after you. No one saw me, but they'll be coming down soon, I bet. Get in quick. What happened to you, Marla?"

"Shot," Wally answered. "We better get her to a hospital before she goes into shock."

Chapter Twenty-Four

Elwa Canyon, above Port Angeles, Washington

As the Suburban barreled down the mountain road toward Port Angeles, Marla's consciousness flickered.

"We've got to get you to a hospital," Wally said.

"No." Her voice was very weak. "Not good for you."

"You're in trouble, lady," said Lucy from the front passenger seat.

"Take me to Colin's house, please—" Marla lapsed into silence. Fresh blood continued to seep from her tattered shirt as she mumbled directions. "Right turn at the first stop sign you get to. Colin will know how to help me and it gets you off the road to town."

The right turn wound through the hilly upland of the Port Angeles basin. They passed a college campus and the sculpted entrance of an art center with a dizzying view of the shoreline far below.

The house was a one story West Coast shack on a modest tree-lined lane. A thin, well-built man with close-cropped hair met them at the door. His face showed alarm as he watched two strangers lifting a bloody form from the back seat. Recognizing Marla, he glared at Wally.

"They're friends, Colin," Marla croaked. "They saved my life. Lighten up. I'll be fine. It's only a gunshot wound." She attempted to stand as he rushed toward her and caught her as she passed out.

"You better keep moving." Marla's voice was soft; she reclined on a tattered sofa. Wrapped in a Navajo blanket and sipping hot tea, she winced as Colin dabbed her wound with iodine. "Head east for a mile till you get to Commercial Street. Take a left. That will drop you back to the Sequim road ... and I'm keeping the fixture." Marla managed a goofy smile as she spoke.

Chapter Twenty-Five

Port Angeles, Washington

A sense of freedom caught the pair as they headed toward the highway aimed at home. Wally's bravado kicked back in as he repeated the story of the left-hand channel pummel.

"Yes, sir, a first descent. Maybe they'll name a rapid after me—"

"Oh, fuck you," Lucy managed an exasperated grin. "Just get us to Camano Island."

"How about The Wally Crack ... Winchester's Gully... John Henry's Hell Hole ... Frank Lloyd's Left ... Camanoman's Crunch ... Gustav Gulch—"

"How about Marla-Saves-Your-Sorry-Ass Canyon?" Lucy asked, anxious to put an end to the escalating list.

The road east from Port Angeles was a four lane undivided thoroughfare lined by tourist businesses and snack bars.

They crested a hill at the 40 mile-per-hour limit and entered a section of truck repair garages and low industrial pole buildings with small-windowed offices flanking truck-sized loading doors. Along the gravel-covered shoulder they passed a parked pickup truck. Three large men stood smoking cigarettes and looking at the traffic.

"Fuck. There's still people watching the highway, and I think they just spotted this Suburban." Looking into the side mirror, Wally watched the figures scrambling into the dark, big-wheeled Ford pickup.

At the top of the hill the pickup dropped out of view. Wally stomped the pedal and accelerated around the gentle down-sloped curve. Eighty miles an hour pushed the roadside into a blur. Lucy grabbed her buckle from behind and snapped it. The speeding Ford pickup was briefly reflected in the mirror but vanished as they shot over another hill. Wally zigzagged the Suburban around the thickening traffic.

"We're never going to lose the Ford, they're all cowboys out here," Wally yelled. "Maybe we'll get stopped by a cop before we get to Sequim."

A low brick structure came into view over the next long curve into yet another valley. A single object sat in front, next to the door. From his speeding viewpoint behind the steering wheel, Wally recognized the shape from 200 yards away as they roared along. A frown wrinkled Wally's already frantic brow. He hit the brakes as they drove by it and locked the Suburban into a sliding, gravel-spitting skid and shuddered to a dusty stop 15 yards beyond.

"Go, go on! What are you doing?" Lucy was incredulous, then incensed as she recognized the object that stopped their flight.

"Do you know what that is, Lucy? It's a drop-arm spindle chair! Unbelievable!"

Wally came to his senses in moments. The Suburban was in drive and he goosed it into a right turn, tucking the vehicle behind the industrial structure. They entered the back parking yard, filled with stacks of hardwood pallets and a loading dock, hidden from the road.

"That's a Gustav Stickley. Do you know how rare that model is?"

"Asshole." Lucy sat, stone-faced, arms crossed and staring forward.

"Maybe I lost them. I wonder what he wants for the chair. It looked original. I can tell that brown."

"And maybe now we're trapped," Lucy said as acid ate into her English brogue. She turned backward, as if expecting to see the dark shape of the Ford upon them.

"Pass me the baseball cap, would ya, honey?" Wally asked. He mentally measured the cargo space left next to the tabletop.

"You're nuts, you know," Lucy hissed as she handed Wally the hat.

"It'll only take a second. Sit here and keep out of sight." Wally stepped out and closed the driver's door quietly.

"Where's Yvgeney?" Lucy asked the heavens.

Wally walked carefully along the west side of the warehouse, carefully peeking around the corner at the highway and the front parking area. No dark Ford pickup, he thought. No pursuit at all. Maybe I lost them when I pulled around back. Next to the Morris chair, the door to the tiny office was wide open.

The chair sat 10 feet in front of the window's vertical gray metal façade. Twenty-two vertical square spindles dropped from the sharply angled paddle of the arm and ended in a stretcher near the ground. The dark, ammonia-stained finish gave it an ancient cast. He glanced at the back of the arms, looking for fat dowels holding the back in place—a Gustav Stickley trademark. They were there as he'd hoped. What luck, he thought. It's the real thing, right as rain. Keeping a wary eye on the four lane on his left, he scooted along the corrugated wall, ducking into the open door. He fingered the cash in his pocket trying to subtract the thousand he gave away on the Black Ball ferry truck deck. Six or seven hundred left, he figured. I bet a hundred dollars gets it.

No evidence of the business inside graced the stained, grimy walls. A single metal chair from some barbershop line of chrome was the only furniture. Wally approached a door that stood slightly ajar. "Hello?" he asked.

The door to the warehouse opened. Ed Brown stood beside it with a smile and a gun.

"Recognize the chair, stupid?"

The Morris chair. Wally smacked himself on the head. "Looks like one I found in the Midwest. I thought I recognized the bird-shit on the arm."

"That's the one you screwed me out of at St. Charles."

"You didn't find the chair." Wally protested. "I did. You just pointed out a new truckload of antiques at the flea market. You were too busy selling that Amish quilt."

"And you bought me a six-pack of beer as a finder's fee and you borrowed the money to do it. It cost me four grand to get that chair back. And two broken fingers for the crook who wouldn't sell it."

"He was a collector, not a crook. The guy was a surgeon, for chrissakes."

"He's a left-handed surgeon, now," Brown said, laughing. He looked Wally over, focused on his hands. "And by the way, have you washed your hands today? Disposing of bodies is messy enough without wondering what disgusting things they've touched."

"Am I clean? I've been up to my neck in the fucking Elwa River all morning, asshole, thanks to you."

193

Brown smiled in a way that made Wally shiver. "I'll take that as a *yes*."

"You *put* that chair out there to *catch me*?"

"It worked. The bait's been out there since you got past my people at the ferry," Ed said. "I've had to chase away three dealers and seventeen tourists thinking it was a yard sale. Where's the British girl?"

"She drowned in the rapids."

"That makes five dead up there this morning." Ed said. His face darkened. "I lost four good men up there today, you fuck. Haven't you done enough?"

The open barrel of a Dirty Harry .44 caliber pistol loomed before Wally's chest.

"Me? You've killed half the antique dealers in British Columbia."

"One more to go."

Lucy was antsy. She had nearly drowned in the river, someone had tried to kidnap her, drive her off a mountain road, and shot at her from a boat. Not to mention the most unpleasant ocean ride of her life. She was heartbroken and pissed off about losing Yvgeney and she was sick to death with the obsession for Mission oak. "I've had it!" she said to no one. Infuriated, she stepped out of the car into the shadows behind the industrial building, headed for the front to find Wally and drag him home. As she turned the corner she saw the black pickup. She pulled back, watching, as two large men stepped out and entered the office. *I have to find Wally and warn him.* Dashing back in the direction of the parked Suburban, she looked for another door.

Wally ignored the gun, arguing with Brown about who found the Morris chair, until the street door opened and two men with the looks of unemployed loggers about them walked inside.

"We lost 'em, boss."

"No, he's here. I caught him. Gentlemen, meet the late Walter Winchester."

"Want us to take him for a ride?"

"No, thanks, boys. I'll finish him here. My associates and I can handle it just fine. In fact, I'm looking forward to it. Take the afternoon off. There's a big bonus in your paychecks this week."

Lucy saw a light in a second floor window. A dumpster under it offered her a perch to look inside. Using a wooden pallet as a ladder, she climbed onto the metal lid and quietly peered over the window sill. Two men locked in an intense conversation sat in a sparely-furnished office with posters of castles on the walls. When she recognized the German in the white coat her heart sank. *They're here. Wally's walked into a trap. I've got to warn him.*

Her foot struck a loose hinge on the dumpster lid, and the metal *clanged* as she scrambled to the ground. She flattened herself to the wall beside it and saw the window above darken as a figure blocked the inside light. She ran.

They were alone again, Ed's gun aimed at Wally's chest. "I'm glad you're still alive, Wally. You get to see some of the things I've made. I'm sure you'll be impressed with what I've accomplished. It will fill your head with my cleverness. You can tell God all about it."

The guy's lost it, Wally thought. He wondered if he could use that against him when the chips were down. Part of his brain said oh goody at the thought of seeing some world-class fakes, but it was quickly stepped on by fear.

Brown motioned Wally toward the back of the building. He waved the long-barreled pistol like a wand.

Wally saw madness in the gesture. He tried to incorporate the observation in his escape plan, but realized he didn't have one. His mind was full of dead ends.

The warehouse was a large pole-building box with high, soundproofed ceilings and mercury halide lights. As they entered, a dog barked from the shadows, followed by a second growl. "Shut up, you curs!" Brown shouted. "I hate those Dobermans," he said to Wally as if the men were two buddies on a stroll. "My partners say we need them."

A series of large crates sat unopened near the freight dock door at the rear. The rest of the interior looked like a museum. One entire wall was fashioned into two-foot- wide cubbyholes, tall and deep enough to hold large paintings. Ornate carved and gilded period frames occupied most of the slots. A group of marble statues, some missing arms and genitals, stood majestically in the center of the chamber. A crème patina suggested antiquity. The workmanship was stunning, reminding Wally of Michelangelo's *Pieta* in its precision and grace.

"We placed a terra-cotta sculpture in the Metropolitan Museum last spring. Etruscan, about sixth century BC, they figured. Fooled all the Italian experts and they're still bragging about having scored it for four-point-two-million dollars from the estate of a countess."

Ed pointed to a large, weathered plaster bust of George Washington. "That one is a joke on forgers," he boomed. "A charming hero of a forger named Durig. Made it in the 30s and even managed to get it presented to President Hoover using a Swiss diplomat as a middleman. It ended up at a convention hall in New Jersey as sort of a national joke, but it disappeared during World War II and that's the point of our brilliant plan. Lots of things are rumored to be around or about to be found or have been simply lost, like this plaster head here. It won't be that valuable to us in a sale, maybe 60 grand, depending on how it's … ah …discovered … but the point is that people expect it to turn up some day and here it is. Brand new, but they won't know that. It might even make it to an Americana sale in New York."

Wally marveled at the surface treatment. Chips and cracks and random hand marks made it easy to believe 80 years of oxygen and carbon dioxide and sulfur dioxide and human contact had created this warm glow.

"Want to see some early Gus?"

Though mindful of the gun at his back, Wally moved toward neatly stacked oak furniture near the small back door to the rear. His survival impulse was severely compromised by the lure of great objects beckoning to him.

"What do you think of the Eastwood chair?"

In all his 25 years of picking, Wally had never run across an Eastwood chair for sale. A nagging suspicion that he'd left one on Martha's Vineyard had bugged him for years. A California dealer at the Expo offered one a year earlier, but it had been refinished and was unsigned. The dealer wanted 30,000 bucks. The example in the warehouse was pristine. Four massive posts of nut-brown oak formed the bulky structure of the impressive chair. Broad thick arms and stretchers bristled with construction details.

"Nineteen-o-two, according to the ink stamp. Want to see it?"

Wally did. The little rush at the sight of a red Stickley stamp with the signature in a box design was definitely preferable to the thoughts about his impending death. He tipped the chair and scanned the underside of the left arm, knowing where to look. It wasn't there. He looked under the other arm.

"It's on the back stretcher, idiot," giggled Brown.

Wally frowned as he set the heavy front legs down. He found the little stamp on the outside surface of the massive rear brace. It made him smile. Finally, some defensive tactics started trickling into his head.

"1902 Eastwood chairs are always signed under the arm. Didn't you know that, Ed? I thought you knew what you were doing."

Ed Brown's face turned red, then a shade of purple.

"What are you talking about? This chair is perfect. It would fool anyone, even an expert."

"Stickley always placed the stamp on the early Eastwood chairs himself and he always chose the arm." Wally really didn't have a plan, but his correction seemed to be putting the cocky auctioneer right up the wall, so he went with it.

"I saw it in a magazine article. They say that once Gus turned it over to the production line, they stamped them anywhere they felt like, that's why most are marked on the stretchers. You'd never find the 1902 mark on a stretcher. Gus wouldn't have placed it there. This chair would get laughed at a real auction." He emphasized *real*.

Brown looked angry and confused. "Under the arm … damn."

Wally sensed that he was pushing Brown too far.

"Is that a Stickley water closet? No shit. I've heard that Gus had them in his New York City house, but I never figured to see one. I used to collect bathroom stuff back East. Did I ever tell you about the time I found an original Shaker Village three-hole outhouse?"

"You sold me that foul contraption, you bastard. Promised me the Shaker collectors would pay big money to own it. You know that. And it cost me 700 dollars to get it shipped to the West Coast. I was stuck with that filthy toilet for seven years. I finally had to get the whole thing steam cleaned so I could stand touching it. There's another reason to kill you."

"Yeah, but wasn't it cool?"

Brown was flustered. He pointed back to the water closet. "Look at the construction."

Wally inspected the rectangular oak tank fastened to the wall. "Nice work in the joints, Ed," Wally said. He realized that the longer he talked, the longer he would stay alive. "I even like the water stains on the side around the pipe. That's a clever touch."

A hammered copper water pipe extended from the bottom and formed an L-shape near the floor. The chain with the acorn handle sported Gustav's oval-and-circle design.

"Nice touch with the chain. I wouldn't have thought of it."

"That's because this is the real one. We've made fifteen just like it. We're going to find them in an old hotel in Biloxi, Mississippi. Should bring a hundred grand, I'm told."

"No kidding! This is the real one? Wow." Wally couldn't help it. He wanted to give it a rub for luck.

"Signed?"

"Just the compass stamp on the acorn pull, and on the drain pipe at eye level."

Good old Gus. The guy had style.

"Did you ever hear of the stash of Frank Lloyd Wright chairs from the Imperial Hotel in Japan?" Brown asked as he prodded Wally toward the back wall. "Rumor has it that hundreds of these chairs were sold for about a dollar apiece when they tore down the hotel in the 60s." Brown was on a roll again. Wally nodded, encouraging the rant. "They're over here. Five dozen of them, brand new. We gave them a patina that suggested 50 years in a hotel dining room. We plan to ship them over there and find them in an abandoned warehouse damaged by the Kobe earthquake."

He stepped to the side as he walked. "Don't step in the dog shit and track it around, Winchester. The place is dirty enough. Fucking Dobermans. I ought to shoot them, too."

He pointed out a group of side chairs hanging neatly from dowels protruding from the wall. Four columns of Prairie School-style chairs were displayed in vertical lines like an art installation.

"Goddamn Germans," Brown confided. "They're so anal, everything has to be exactly in its place." He bungled a sarcastic attempt at a German accent.

Wally looked down at the excrement. "They look like Maher designs," he said. A plan was quickening.

Brown laughed, "They're Elmslie. It's obvious. I thought you were smarter than that."

"Look at the top rail, Ed." Wally gestured toward the chairs. Brown turned his head. "See how the ends hang over the back?"

Still talking as Brown inspected the chair, Wally bent as if to tie his shoe and scooped up some of the foul pile on the floor. "No, you're right," he said as he stood up. "They're more like Maher."

"Of course I'm right."

Using his left hand, Wally rubbed his nose and faked a sneeze, watching Brown's frown as he wiped it on his pant leg. He hid his cupped right hand, holding the dog dirt, behind his leg. He was remembering long road trips and Brown's obsession with filth and body fluids. Wally knew it was a lame plan but it was all he had.

Brown was bragging about his partners. "They'd been at this business for years before I met them on my second Europe trip. They've got experts for everything. We got a guy up in Port Alberni now ... making Stradivarius guitars, for chrissake. Two million apiece, we figure."

"Ed, who was it they found floating in your acid bath?" Wally was running out of reasons to stay alive.

"Mitchell."

"Moose Mitchell. You killed Moose? We were buddies. We all drove across the country together."

"I needed someone about my size and build. Moose was losing his good looks, actually. He had nothing else to live for. I did him a favor. I just stuck my wallet in his back pocket, my wedding ring on his finger, and let him rot for a couple of days in the acid."

Brown's true madness shone in his wandering, unfocused eyes. Wally sensed the chitchat was over. "I just want to shake your hand, congratulate you," he said and reached out with his cupped right hand.

Brown instinctively brought up his hand and stopped. His smile was evil. "Did you wash your—?" It was too late.

Wally's feces-coated fingers grabbed the auctioneer's hand before he could withdraw it. Cold slime of Doberman excrement squished between their fingers as Wally squeezed the auctioneer's hand firmly.

Brown looked down in horror and began to scream. "What have you done? You've soiled me!" He stared down at his sticky, dog-fouled palm in disbelief. A movement alerted him and he looked up in time to see, but not stop, Wally's slimy touch.

Brown choked and sputtered from the horror of the putrid odor filling his nose and throat and the terrible stinging in his wide-open eyes. As he tried to clear his vision, a sharp impact on his wrist knocked the gun to the floor. Wally kicked it under an oak settee. Brown lunged, shrieking. Wally held his attacker back with a Mackintosh bedroom chair, smearing feces on the beautifully faked white lacquer leg.

Brown ripped the chair away from Wally's slippery hand, searching madly for something lethal. The auctioneer grabbed the back bar from a Mission recliner. Its seat back fell, clattered onto the cement floor.

Wally back-pedaled into the empty corner as Brown advanced, holding the chair bar in front of him as a cudgel. With a final burst of rage, he pinned Wally to the wall, pressing the oak rod against his throat.

The pressure was unbearable. Brown's wild, dung-smeared face was inches from Wally's. He lost his grip on the bar as his air supply dwindled. Stars sparkled and he smelled the shit. The light dimmed.

Lucy carefully approached the street side again and saw the black pickup was gone. A man stood by the front door. Her heart stopped. It was Yvgeney. Stifling a scream of surprise she ran 10 steps into his arms. "Oh my god," she whispered. "You're alive." Her hand went to his face. She pushed back his unruly cowlick and felt hair matted over a wound behind his ear. "You're hurt."

"I am fine."

"What happened to you? How did you find us? The man said you were dead."

"I will tell you later." Yvgeney pulled her close and kissed her mouth. "I have to help our friend."

"How can I help?"

"You can go back to the Suburban and wait."

"We're in this mess together," she argued, not letting go.

"If I worry about your safety, I will be of no use to Wally. Please go and be safe and let me work."

"I love you," she said.

"Later. Now go."

Lucy turned and stumbled toward the rear parking area. She watched the man she'd always dreamed she'd find turn away and disappear through the front door.

Yvgeney entered the warehouse through the office and was surprised at the grandness in the room. Amazing objects here was his first thought. Scuffling and grunts took his attention to the opposite corner where two figures were locked in a struggle.

Yvgeney sprinted across the room. He had no weapon. As he ran through aisles of antiquities, he saw Wally pinned against the outside wall, as Brown, very much alive, tried to crush Wally's windpipe with brute force and a length of wood. Yvgeney scanned the warehouse and saw no one else.

Yvgeney analyzed the situation as he ran. He had no weapon. At least one adversary. Two exit doors, one to the rear, one he had just walked through. More closed doors were visible behind a balcony railing above him. A staircase reached it from the opposite wall.

He yelled to the auctioneer and scooped up a round, red enamel box from a shelf. Diamonds, blue stones, and gold filigree danced on its ornate gold and platinum hinges.

"Hey, what is this? It looks like Faberge. Hey, auction man."

Brown's face was a mask of rage. He pressed harder on Wally's throat. Wally's hands held it back, but he was nearly gone. His eyes rolled upward slowly.

Yvgeney opened the elaborately articulated egg and heard a lovely song, complete with tiny gold and silver automatons skating around a circle of Baccarat ice.

The box's familiar music rattled Brown's psyche. He hesitated.

The Russian dropped the enameled jewel onto the cement floor and watched it bounce a bit and stop, lid open to tiny skaters. He brought his heel down hard and felt the soft metal flatten against broken glass and jewels.

"Stop that!" Brown screamed. "That's half a million dollars. It took three months to make that egg!" He released his hold on the bar. Wally slid to the floor and tipped over, gagging and retching. Brown spit at Wally's crumpled form and turned to face Yvgeney.

Yvgeney found his weapons. He reached over to the cubbyhole slots and pulled out the first painting his hand fell on. It was dark, a Flemish-style portrait of the holy family. Gold halos glowed in the mercury halide light. Craquelure covered the 17th century surface. It was obvious to the investigator's eye that it was superb, even if it wasn't right.

"What is this ... a Rubens? What a lovely treatment of the Christ child." Yvgeney lifted the painting by its ornate frame with both hands and slammed it down onto a tall oak magazine stand. The canvas ripped. Yvgeney left it hanging like a broken necklace. He hoped to hell the painting had not been an original. He would never live with himself later.

The auctioneer began to scream again and advanced toward the shelves of art.

Yvgeney, eyes locked on the auctioneer's advance, reached out sideways and felt another frame. He pulled it out. Brown stopped.

"And what is this one?" Yvgeney asked. He glanced down at the dark portrait of a bare-chested woman in his hands. "Let me guess ... Renoir?"

"Put that down," Brown wailed. He walked, his stride almost wooden, toward the Russian.

Yvgeney raised it over his head, ready to smash it like the Rubens.

Automatic weapon fire reverberated around the warehouse.

Yvgeney spotted a figure standing on the balcony looking down, a Kalashnikov in his hand. "That will be enough of the object breaking," he said. Yvgeney knew him. The ruddy German sneer had been the last image in his brain as he hit the water in the dark Port Angeles night. His head still ached but that was the least of his problems now.

"Put the painting down, Russian. I thought I saw the last of you on a ferry the other night. You must have a hard head and the gills of a fish."

"Russian Navy, 10 years."

"Figures. Mr. Brown, don't stand in my line of fire. Get over by the wall." The lopsided grin was back on the auctioneer's face. He sauntered over to the corner.

The automatic barked a volley of gunfire.

Still holding the painting, Yvgeney watched the auctioneer's smile turn wrong as bullets struck him. Eyes wide and incredulous, Brown looked down at the red stains on his neatly pressed shirt. He took two small steps, still grinning oddly, and sagged to the floor near Wally.

"We didn't want any rounds hurting the paintings, you understand."

The blonde German held the gun on Yvgeney and walked down the stairs to the concrete floor. "I was hoping that the antique dealer would win and save me some work." He advanced cautiously as he spoke. "The auctioneer's madness and the mess you people started made him a liability."

Yvgeney held the painting in front of him like a canvas shield. He could not help but admire the workmanship on the frame. *This really is a second-rate Renoir.* Looking up from the canvas, he glimpsed movement in the shadows under the balcony behind the German. Another voice, one Yvgeney did not recognize, spoke from above them. A cascade of German made the blonde gunman shrink back, fear on his face. A shot rang out. Claus the blonde German fell to his knees and toppled over. A hole in his throat spurted blood. He quivered for a moment and lay still.

Yvgeney searched the room for the killer. He saw movement above as another figure walked down the stairs to the warehouse floor. The voice was not familiar, and Yvgeney could not make out the face. He sized up his new adversary's slight build and weapon.

"You will have to put the painting down now, my friend. It is one of the real ones, a Renoir, but not one of his best. Do you agree, art detective? Claus, the idiot, would have destroyed it just to get to you. He was proud of his … expertise, and you have embarrassed him two days in a row." The German … Austrian? … accent thickened as he narrowed the distance. He sighed. "Too bad we have to …" he hesitated, as if searching for the right word, "re-shuffle our personnel." He laughed at his choice and said, "I am afraid our North American operations have come to an end."

Yvgeney glanced down at the portrait. He turned it around, holding it between him and the German.

"There has been enough damage to our enterprise," the man continued, drawing closer. "Please, would you stand over by your friend? This gun jumps all over the place and you are in front of two Tintorettos and a long-lost Picasso."

Yvgeney recognized the face. The mustachioed fellow from the auction, the camper. *Of course, the character with the smallest part in the play.* He chided himself for not seeing it. "So you are the brains," he said, stalling. He held the painting close to his chest but saw no way out.

"Move it, or I will shoot you through the painting. I never liked it. I can always make another Renoir. Do it for the safety of the art. That is your job, no? Put the painting down and join your friend. Die like a man."

Another movement from the shadows behind the stairs caught Yvgeney's eye. He recognized Lucy, creeping forward, a sword in her hands. Unaware, the German sighed resolutely, and aimed at Yvgeney.

Lucy stepped on a piece of broken plaster. The subtle crunch caught the German's attention. He cocked his head.

Yvgeney acted. "Wait!" he shouted. "I need to know something."

"Your days of knowing are at an end."

"Please, answer one question. It has been baffling me a long time."

"Why should I bother to enlighten you before you die?"

"If the movie of my life is about to end, let me resolve this question. You have all the control in your hands." Yvgeney watched Lucy creep closer. He had no other tools. "What did Smith think was so funny back in Port Alberni?"

"He was still speaking about the auction when I killed him. Smashed his skull. Broke his neck. It was easy. He was an old man."

"Winchester told me Smith had a chisel in his chest when he saw the body in the van. In that Walmart lot." Yvgeney dared not look at Lucy and give her away.

"That was window dressing. For the police to find. One of the American's tools."

"What did Smith think was so funny?" Yvgeney asked again.

"The auction was a sham. Everyone in the room knew it … except you two. You and your bungling friend."

"The press also?"

"All we needed was the fellow from the antiques magazine, the one from Maine, to record that the matter was over. Smith's foolhardy junket exposing the desk could be forgotten and we could continue our enterprise under the radar."

"The cameraman, the TV crew, the newspaper reporter?"

"Our men."

"So it is safe to assume you are not an antique dealer from Maine?" Yvgeney stalled.

"The closest I have been to Maine was eating a lobster in Boston. I enjoyed the sound the creature made when it was dropped into boiling water."

Yvgeney said, "Hey, Shultz, do you like to watch old movies? I do."

The German sighted down the barrel. "My name is not Shultz, it is Holtzman. Do not give me any more of that New Age babble, dead man." His head tilted again at a new sound behind him.

Yvgeney stepped forward toward the barrel of the revolver, aimed now at his face. Holtzman cocked the hammer. "Stop right there."

With his eyes on the trigger, Yvgeney threw the Renoir to the floor, smashing the frame. "Now!" he shouted.

Lucy lunged from behind the German, holding the long blade in both hands, and thrust it forward.

Great surprise filled the German's face as the weapon plunged into his back. He seemed suddenly unconcerned. Behind him, Lucy looked at Yvgeney through wide-open eyes. Her face was a blank mask of resolve.

"Yank the blade up, Lucy!" Yvgeney reached for Holtzman's gun hand as his focus cleared. The pistol fired wildly as Holtzman tried to turn.

Lucy pulled up on the hilt. Flesh gave way as the blade traveled deeper. Holtzman pitched forward, dropping the gun. She let go of the jewel-encrusted handle as he fell. He twitched on the floor as lights in his eyes dimmed.

Yvgeney lifted the painting and noticed the canvas was not torn. He whispered "Thank you" and stepped over broken gesso to embrace Lucy. "You are a hero, little one, you saved my life. Thank you."

"That makes us even. I couldn't lose you twice, sweetheart, now could I?"

Wally struggled, rose from the floor, stepped over Brown's body without a glance. His voice raspy, he said, "Do you think if we drop the back seat we can move the table forward and get that Morris chair in the Suburban?"

Chapter Twenty-Six

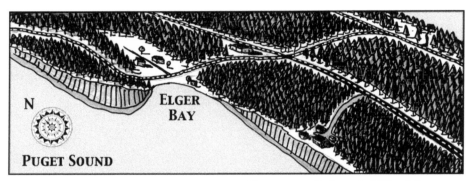

Camano Island, Washington

Steam rose from Yvgeney's arm as he lifted it out of the water and hugged Lucy's bare shoulders. In the twilight sky behind her, gray clouds threatened rain. He sipped red wine from a tulip glass. "Did you read anything in the morning paper about a police raid on the clock shop?" he asked as he moved closer to sniff her hair. "My Interpol chatter tells me there has been an action."

"They don't often report Canadian news down here, my dear."

Rae, elbows on the cedar tub rim, turned to Wally, beside her, and said, "A clock shop? You told me you were writing a story and antiquing."

"I was looking for something, a gift for you," Wally lied.

"That's so thoughtful of you, Wally. Where is it?"

"I didn't like the workmanship—too crude."

"What's this about a police raid? Were you in danger?"

Yvgeney said, "There was a break-in."

Two glasses later, Yvgeney said, "Good choice of that boat, Wally. That Boston Whaler. I was glad we had a flat bottom when we hit that fog."

"You went boating?" Rae asked. "That sounds like fun. I would have gone if I'd known it was that kind of trip. When I'm with you, Wally, you spend all our time swapping stories in dirty old furniture stores."

"I caught a salmon," Lucy told her. "He got away and I was glad."

"Fishing, too? Next thing I know you'll tell me you went white water rafting."

Lucy opened her mouth to speak, but Yvgeney closed it with a kiss. She persisted. "You still haven't told me how you found us in Port Angeles, after you ..." she hesitated, seeing Yvgeney's head nod imperceptibly toward Rae, "met that German man."

"It was painful to be separated from you so close to shore. After I got my bearings, it was a piece of cake after ten years swimming in the Arctic Sea. The only hard part was finding you."

"And your buddy, Wally," Wally said.

"Yes, Wally, I wanted to find you also. Actually, it was you who told me where to wait. Renting a car, I started a widening search spiral, just like on Vancouver Island. It took nine hours until I saw that chair, some kilometers to the east. Then I settled down and waited across the road."

Rae looked at the strange man who had arrived with Wally and Lucy the day before and said, "Wait a minute. Did you just say you jumped off a ferry boat?"

"Just showing off," Yvgeney said. "It is an old Russian Navy tradition."

Under the water, Lucy's feet explored his ankles. "What's this?"

"That bump on my leg? I hurt my self, years ago when I was learning how to jump off moving trains. I was good at it ... eventually. I could leave a train at 30 kilometers an hour and still keep my feet."

"I thought you were a Navy man," Lucy said.

"My military training could be called thorough."

"Mystery man," Lucy said and snuggled under his arm.

The lights of a neighboring island twinkled on the horizon.

Rae said to Wally, "I'm going on the next road trip with you if you're going to make it that interesting. Just promise you take a more reliable vehicle, something like that Suburban you borrowed."

"Rae, honey, if I drag you into a big adventure, I promise next time I'll be prepared."

"Deal," she said.

"That reminds me," Wally said, as the last of the sunset leaked under the cloudbank. Yellow light in the cabin window fell on the bark-covered legs of the dining set. "Yvgeney, I hear you're going into the flea market business. Welcome aboard."

"That was, as you say, *pillow talk*. Lucy wants to open a stall in Paris, at the famous Clignancourt Market, no less. She thinks I can use my Russian status to pick Havana for 50s things. I find them, she sells them."

"When you get to Cuba, find me a marshmallow couch, OK?"

"I will give you first shot at it." The Russian smiled.

Wally smiled, too. "You're learning capitalism way too fast, Yvgeney."

"I learned it from the best." Yvgeney said. "You know, Wally, my friend, when you finally get your van back you really ought to cover that sideboard with a coat of shellac. It will kill that strong Canadian fragrance."

Wally considered the lingering memory of Don Smith decaying in the darkness of a Walmart parking lot. He gazed across Puget Sound's cold water and smiled. "Can't touch it, Yvgeney. That's the original finish."

Jack Gunter is a prominent Pacific Northwest writer, artist, and antique dealer who specializes in twentieth century decorative arts.

With a degree in biology and graduate training in organic chemistry, he was teaching school in Massachusetts in 1973 when he wrote and illustrated his first book, "The Gunter Papers," which he describes as a futuristic junior high school science curriculum.

A self taught artist using the ancient technique of egg tempera painting, he exhibited his large format works in several New England museums and was included in an Andrew Wyeth and Family show in the Sharon, N.H. Art Center in 1979. That year a studio fire claimed all of his existing paintings and landed him in Washington State with a pick up truck, his dog, and the clothes on his back, relocating because in Puget Sound he was the only person in a thousand mile radius who wanted mission oak objects and the Northwest was chock full of Mr. Stickley's furniture.

Since moving to Camano Island he has created over one thousand additional paintings, three movies as a SAG indie filmmaker, and four books -- an illustrated guide to Northwest history narrated by a flying pig and three novels in the Wally Winchester adventure series.

He lives in a cliffside cabin with views of the Olympic Mountains, eagles, and spouting whales out his front window.

CPSIA information can be obtained
at www.ICGtesting.com
Printed in the USA
FFHW021435050719
53407390-59116FF